BITTEN
BY
DARKNESS

Editing by Chris St. John
Cover design by Nichole Wolfe
Formatting template by Derek Murphy

Visit the author's website at www.nicholewolfe.com

Printed in the United States of America

First Printing: 2021

ISBN 978-1-7372749-0-2

THE FORBIDDEN FATE SERIES

BITTEN BY DARKNESS

NICHOLE WOLFE

This book is dedicated to:

My parents, who nurtured my love of books
My husband, who didn't think this was a crazy dream
My children, who make this crazy dream worth it

NEWSLETTER SIGNUP

You can get a free e-book copy of BITTEN BY DARKNESS to keep on your favorite e-reader device by signing up for my newsletter at www.nicholewolfe.com. My newsletter subscribers are the first to see covers, videos, and other behind-the-scenes. See you there!

If you're already signed up for my newsletter, thank you! I hope you enjoy your free e-book and stay tuned for more updates, discounts, and exclusive giveaways.

CHAPTER ONE

I HATE THIS PLACE. CHARLIE SIGHED AS HE GAZED UP AT THE mansion he once called home. Not that it had ever felt like home. Ever.

He swept through the fresh layer of snow that covered the walkway leading to the large, double French doors. Solar lights dotted the path, and the marble columns on each side of the entrance loomed above him. It was a pretty picture that hid the horror within. He took a deep breath, preparing himself for the task at hand.

Pushing his way through the doors, he stepped into the grand foyer. A long, red carpet ran along the marble floor and up the winding staircase. He barely made it through the door before a slave came and insisted on taking his bags. Charlie nodded, squinting at the balding man who crouched to pick up his heavy suitcase.

"Paul? Is that you?"

The man gave him a wide grin. "Good to have you back, Master Charles."

Charlie gaped at him. "Hell, you've gotten old. I barely recognized you." He'd spent the last decade surrounded by the ancient, but ageless. Paul's thinning grey hair was a shocking reminder that time had certainly marched on.

Paul laughed, a hearty sound that brightened the gloomy mood Charlie had been carrying around with him since he'd received his Maker's summons to return home. "And I see you haven't aged one bit, sir."

"Being undead will do that."

"Wait until I tell Nessie you've returned. She'll be so surprised." Paul huffed as he lugged the suitcase across the room towards the stairs.

Nessie. Gods, how he'd missed that child. She was the one thing that made him not dread returning to this wretched place. He remembered sitting in the study for hours as he'd listen to her tell fantastical tales of adventure. One of her favorite stories had been Peter Pan. "You'd make a perfect Peter," she'd chirp. "You never get older." Even now, he smiled at the memory of the lively little girl. Almost made him forget all the horrid things he'd had to do during his never-ending service to his Maker.

"Charlie, my boy!"

He ground his molars. Speak of the devil. Jacques swooped into the room, clapping him on the shoulder. A vivid picture of punching the bastard in the nose crossed his mind. Instead, he managed a smile and hoped his face cooperated. The grin on Jacques' pale face told him he managed well enough.

"How did we do at council?" At least Jacques wasted little

time on niceties. Straight to the point. Thank the gods. Less time he had to pretend to smile. His Maker often sent Charlie to take care of the tedious negotiations at council. If he received the council's approval, he returned to Jacques to notify him of the success.

"Well, sir. The council seems quite interested in your proposal to expand the blood and slave markets across seas." Charlie's gut churned. It had become common practice to use human slaves again after the "supernaturals" had come out into the open. The practice never sat well with him, having fought in the American Civil War four centuries earlier. He had survived the hell of battle only to dive headfirst into the pit a few short years later. Thanks to the son of a bitch clutching his shoulder like a long-lost friend.

"Excellent, excellent. Took them long enough to decide." Jacques stepped away, crossing the room toward the wet bar. Charlie resisted the urge to wipe his shoulder clean.

"Yes, sir. I apologize for the delay in my return, but-"

Jacques laughed, a cold contrast to Paul's hearty one. "With those old windbags, I'm surprised it didn't take you a century to convince them. And never, ever apologize. It's weak to admit you were wrong. Makes other people question you. And we can't have that, especially now."

"Now, sir?"

"Of course!" Jacques pointed at him. "I expect you to hold down the fort while I'm at council setting up the expansion operations. And these slaves need a firm hand. Hell, even some of the vampires do. Otherwise, they forget who the master is."

It took Charlie a moment to compose himself. Master... of the entire estate? He cleared his throat. "Are you sure, sir? Aren't there more experienced-"

"No, no, no." Jacques shook his head. "You've shown me dedication, loyalty, and quite a sharp mind to deal with the council members. You're the best man for the job. Besides, Kat would be the next eldest, and I'll be damned before I put a woman in charge of my estate. Gods know what I'd come back to!"

"Of... of course, sir. I'm honored to do this service for you," he lied, forcing himself into a small bow. Which pleased Jacques immensely. *Gods, I fucking hate this.* But sacrifices had to be made if he wanted his revenge. *Patience, he'll get what's coming to him soon enough.*

Nessie bolted up in her poor excuse for a bed, groaning as her bracelet vibrated again. *Not ready*, she thought and dozed back off until it became painful. The bracelet was programmed to shock her if she didn't get to where it told her to get to within a certain (short) period of time. She glanced down at the stupid thing, wishing she could tear it from her flesh. Unfortunately, a layer of steel covered the electrical wires, making human fingers too weak to snap it. Another jolt got her to drag herself from beneath the thin blanket, sighing as she saw her bracelet flashing "FEEDING ROOM ONE".

Nessie dragged her feet, wincing as her bracelet shocked her again. She heard her mother fall into step behind her as they entered the room together, and the pain in her wrist finally stopped. For now.

I hate this room. Nessie scowled at the white furniture and rugs. Even the walls were a pale silvery gray. It was the dumbest décor decision as far as a feeding room went. But she didn't make decisions around here. Or any decisions for that matter.

"Don't slouch, Vanessa," her mother chided from behind her.

She narrowed her eyes, ready to stick out her tongue until Master entered the room. Lowering her gaze to the floor, the two of them bowed their heads as he passed them. She noticed a second pair of feet cross in front of her vision a few moments after and her stomach cramped. Logan, the younger male who usually fed from her, had wandering hands and a penchant for sinking his teeth to the bone. Vampires were assholes like that.

"C'mon, I haven't got all day!" Master bellowed as he lounged on the sofa across the room.

She scrambled over to sit on the cushion next to Logan, her eyes focusing on her fiddling hands in her lap. Any moment now he'd snatch up her wrist and dig his ugly fangs into her vein. Her breaths came unevenly, her heart racing, her body bracing for the coming pain.

"You seem uneasy."

Her breath hitched. That wasn't Logan. She recognized that voice. It had once been her favorite voice in the whole world. Her gaze shot up.

It was him. The vampire she had once called friend. Best friend if she was being honest with herself. Before he disappeared on her, never to be seen or heard from for the last ten years. The one who'd left her here to rot like a forgotten piece of garbage. Vampires were assholes like that.

"It's alright." He reached for her hand, which she snatched out of reach without a thought.

His eyebrows raised in surprise.

Shit. Slaves don't behave like that. She hesitated for a moment before holding her arm out, staring at him. His face was exactly as she remembered. Bright blue eyes under thick brows that matched his perfectly styled black hair.

He glanced at her offered hand. "Are you sure?" he asked, shocking the shit out of her. She wouldn't be surprised if her jaw just fell off her face.

"Are you daft, boy? You don't ask her permission. She's a fucking slave, for gods' sakes! What did those council members teach you!" Master's eyes landed on her. "Come here, girl."

The command that made her knees wobble as she crossed the room. Shit, now she'd done it. She couldn't just hand over her hand like a good little slave, could she?

As soon as she was within reach, he snatched her arm. She could already feel it bruising beneath his grasp. He yanked her down onto the unoccupied cushion, his other hand gripping her thigh to hold her in place. As his fangs jabbed into her wrist, she yelped. Even Logan's bite had never been that bad. Like someone jabbing a needle into your vein and twisting. She clenched her teeth as Master took long, painful pulls. Don't cry. Tears are weakness. Thankfully, it didn't last long.

When Master released her, he shoved her off the couch. "There. That's how it's done, boy!"

Her ass landed on the rug. Son of a bitch! Now, there was a big red mark on the floor.

She turned and glanced at Charlie's face, a calm, unreadable mask except for the slight ticking in his jaw. Was he was upset at her ill-treatment or just anxious to get his own taste of her? Probably the latter. She clenched her teeth and picked her sorry ass up off the floor. Might as well get this over with.

The woman glared death at him as she shuffled back across the room. Charlie wanted to throw an identical look at Jacques, the cruel son of a bitch, but he managed to keep his face neutral. Jacques had to think he worshiped his every move, took every barbaric lesson to heart, blackening his soul for the chance at vengeance. But watching his Maker rip into that woman's arm like a savage made him tense with rage. It took serious effort to keep himself from flying across the room and attempting to separate Jacques' fangs from his jaw. Which made no sense. He had witnessed Jacques do far worse over the long years. A nasty bite was child's play for him. Why such a strong reaction now? After all these years? Was his soul crying out for an end to all the depravity?

Sinking back down onto the cushion beside him, the woman's eyes still held a promise of murder. She did not like him, and it showed. As she closed the distance, her scent wafted towards him. In a single moment, all thoughts ceased. His mind fogged by the aroma of her sweet-smelling lifeblood. Without thinking, he caressed her hand, lifting it, bringing the taste of paradise closer to his mouth. Nothing mattered but getting her skin against his lips and her blood inside his body. Nothing else mattered. Not him, not Jacques, not even his revenge. This moment. Only this moment had any meaning for him.

He pressed the tip of his tongue against her open vein. The first taste was better than he ever thought possible. It had him clutching her wrist as he sank his fangs into her delicate flesh one inch at a time. As her blood slipped past his tongue, his body flushed. Waves of warmth swept through him. The numbness that kept an icy grip on his body shattered as his heart began beating for the first time in almost four hundred years. He released her wrist on a silent gasp, his eyes snapping open.

As his mind and vision cleared, a deep scowl on her full mouth caught his eye first. With her blood pumping its way straight to his heart, he gazed into the bright hazel eyes of the child he had so missed over the last ten years. A gaze that seemed to reach inside him and put a vice-grip on his warming heart. Recognition slammed into him like a sucker punch to the gut.

Nessie.

Gods, he should have recognized her before. The pale blonde hair of her childhood was gone, replaced by long, honey-colored waves. Her complexion darker than he remembered as if she'd been kissed by sunlight.

Before he had time to take in the new woman that had taken the place of the young girl he so fondly remembered, Jacques snapped from across the room, "You've done your job, girl. Now get out."

Charlie's chest tightened at the reminder that Jacques was still in the room. Clenching her jaw, Nessie bowed her head and swiftly moved toward the exit.

Look back, look back at me.

And she did. With a look that almost froze his heart all over again.

CHAPTER TWO

NESSIE COLLAPSED INTO THE CHAIR AT THE SMALL kitchen table. What a night. Being worked like a slave was grueling enough, but to have two bloodsucking fiends at your wrist in one night. No wonder her legs felt like jelly. Admittedly, the second one had been a tad gentler. Okay, fine. He'd been the gentlest feeding she'd ever experienced. But he was still a fiend! No matter how gently he used those wretched fangs of his.

And the way he'd looked at her when he was finished...the nerve of that guy! Vampires were assholes. Period.

"Drink your tea, Vanessa." Her mother placed a steaming mug in front of her. Nessie wrinkled her nose at the horrid smell. Her mother narrowed her dark, brown eyes on her and pointed at the mug. "Drink."

Her father walked into the room. "Good morning, my lovely young ladies." His eyes drooped and the dark bags under them gave away his weariness, but it couldn't wipe the smile from his face.

Her mother placed a hand on her hip. "I'm hardly a young lady anymore, Paul."

Skipping over to her, his smile widened. "You'll always be young in my eyes, my darling Eva," he said, pecking her on the cheek. She rolled her eyes at him and continued wiping the counters.

Nessie smiled at them. She always loved seeing them together, even if only for a few minutes. Her father pulled his gaze from her mother to look at her. "Speaking of not being young anymore." He wiggled his eyebrows as he pulled a package from under his shirt.

Nessie's face heated. "Dad, you shouldn't have." Her father was one of the few slaves permitted off the estate to gather supplies like food, clothing, and whatever else the Master told him to buy. Which meant her gift had most likely not been on that approved list and her father had risked a lot to get it for her.

Setting the package on the table, he sang a very off-key version of "Happy Birthday," his face glowing. By the second verse, several other slaves crowded the small communal kitchen and joined in.

"Eighteen already. I can't believe it. You're soon gonna have grey hair like me," he said, nudging her with his elbow.

She nudged him back before unfolding the wrapping. Her heart fluttered as her fingers clutched the new notebook and pen. She usually used old napkins or scraps of paper she found crumpled up in trash cans. Glancing up at him, she found tears pooling in his eyes. "I love it," she said, standing to give him a well-deserved hug.

He clutched her back, sniffling. "Well, it was your mother's idea. She said you'd like that."

Nessie glanced over at her mother, her smile faltering. Her mother suggested this perfect gift? Surprising. "Thanks, Mom," she muttered.

Her mother smiled, taking a step towards Nessie and pulling her into a hug. "You're welcome, honey."

Nessie patted her back until her mother released her. Then, she and her father sat back down at the table where she admired her gift. It felt wonderful as she ran her fingers through the crisp, blank pages waiting to be filled.

"Nessie," her father said, making her lift her head. "Drink your tea." He pointed at the untouched mug.

"But, Dad," she whined.

He chuckled. "Don't 'but, Dad' me. Drink."

Nessie groaned, grabbing the mug and chugging the nasty liquid down.

Charlie stumbled down the hallway as he struggled to get a handle on the sensations rampaging through him. What the hell was wrong with him? He felt like a fledgling all over again. Only, instead of struggling with the icy cold breaths and widespread numbness, he felt like he was about to combust at any moment. Like fire licked through his veins, spreading from his chest outward. Sleep, he thought. He needed to rest after the long journey from the council. His kind couldn't go more than a few short days without blood and rest, or they'd start deteriorating. Yes, that was it. Gods, please let that be it. Because the alternative...he didn't even want to think about.

"Charles!"

He groaned as a tall, curvy body crashed into him. He'd completely forgotten. Katherine. The vampire lover he'd left behind ten years ago. And hadn't thought about one bit since.

"Oh, how I've missed you," she purred into his ear.

Really? She'd missed him? Doubtful. Their kind rarely felt more than pure lust as far as romance went. Their arrangement had been about satisfying their needs, nothing more. Perhaps she'd missed the attentive lover he'd been, but not him.

His skin crawled as her hands clutched him, and he peeled himself from her embrace. "Not now, Kat."

"What do you mean 'not now'? It's been ten long, lonely years," she moaned, her fingers already gliding under his shirt. "Haven't you missed me?"

Obviously, he'd been spot on about what she really missed. Though, he doubted she'd gone an entire decade without finding another to satisfy her needs. He hadn't.

With his blood rapidly heating with every moment, a quick romp in the sheets might be what he needed. But he couldn't even think of touching her without his stomach churning in protest.

"It's been a long journey. I need to rest." His kind didn't have to sleep every day, but much like humans, too many days without proper rest would have some nasty side effects. He found his suitcase in the closet already emptied. Paul must have already unpacked for him. He smiled at the kind gesture before turning back to find Kat pouting.

He rolled his eyes at her, pulling a pair of boxers from his dresser and heading toward the en suite bathroom.

"I... I could join you in the shower," she called. He threw her a stern look. "Fine." She twirled around, her dark hair flying, and stomped toward the door, turning back to bark at him, "You'll need your rest in order to please me properly anyway."

He sighed as he heard the door slam shut. Peace...for now, at least. Heading for the bathroom, he hoped a cold shower would cool his feverish body.

Nessie tiptoed down the hallway towards her favorite morning spot. She was dying to break open her new notebook. She usually spent the early morning hours reading the wide array of books available in the study and scribbling away her own stories on scraps of paper she rummaged out of the trash. But as the door of the study came into view, she hesitated. Light shone from beneath the door and a faint shadow moved within the strip of light. Who would be up at this hour? Everyone else retired for the day. A pang of disappointment swept through her. She turned to leave whomever it was in peace when the door creaked open.

"You're welcome to come in, Nessie."

She turned back towards the door, her frown deepening. What was Charlie doing up past dawn? "How did you know I was out here?"

He pointed at his ears, smiling.

"Oh, right." Vampire. Duh.

"Actually, I'm glad I ran into you. I wanted to apologize for what happened earlier." He opened the door further, standing in the doorway in nothing but a pair of sweatpants. Her breath caught in her throat. She couldn't not notice all those lean muscles he was showing off so shamelessly.

Her face heated and she forced her eyes away. She should not be ogling someone who drank from her a few hours ago. Even if he felt the need to apologize for it. "No need to apologize. That's my job," she gritted out.

Charlie shuffled his feet, glancing at the floor. "Right. Well, he shouldn't have been so rough---"

Ah, so it was Master's treatment he wanted to apologize for. The same Master she'd dealt with the last ten years? That Master? She snapped her gaze back to him. "I'm used to it."

She saw his throat move, but he hesitated. No response to that slice of truth, huh?

He cleared his throat. "I heard it was your birthday today."

He heard? He couldn't even remember when her birthday was? She shrugged, pursing her lips.

"Well, I wanted to give you something for your birthday, and I remembered how much you liked reading."

She crossed her arms over her chest, raising a brow at him. "I hope you remember that much. You taught me how to read. You know...before you left."

Charlie gazed down at her, the corner of his lip twitching. "Trust me, I remember."

"But you can't remember my birthday on your own?"

He looked taken aback for a moment before he scowled. "Do you remember mine?"

"I would if you'd have ever told me." She stepped towards him, placing a palm on her chest. "I remember important things about my friends."

His face perked up at the last word.

"Or at least those I thought were my friends," she tacked on.

The start of a smile dropped away just as quickly. He shoved his hands in the pockets of his sweatpants, which pulled them down further on his hips. Her gaze latched on to the deep lines of his hip bones and she felt the room hike up a few degrees.

"Anyway," he said. "I thought you might like to pick out a book from the study to keep, perhaps."

She forced her eyes back to his face. A book...of her own? Was he serious? When he held the door open for her to come in, she found her feet shuffling toward the shelves of story after story calling her name.

He followed her like an annoying puppy as she perused the shelves trying to decide which book she wanted to keep forever. Chances like this didn't come along too often for a slave. Decisions, decisions.

"What's this?" he asked, snatching her perfectly untouched notebook from under her arm.

She whipped around, opening her mouth and reaching her hand out to grab the notebook back before stopping herself. *He's a vampire. You're a slave. And he's not your friend anymore.* Which meant she couldn't do anything she wanted around him anymore either. Like smack him. And not playfully like when she was a child. Her fists clenched at her sides.

He quirked his brow, watching her with those unnaturally blue eyes. His lips curved in a smirk, as if amused by her barely-restrained retaliation. She growled under her breath, crossing her arms over her chest and looking anywhere but at him. When she heard him chuckle, she wanted to stab him with her pen. But it was new, and she didn't want it covered in blood, so she resisted.

He opened the notebook, the scrap pieces of her writing falling out. And she'd just organized those, too. *Don't stab him. Don't stab him.* When he picked up the pieces and began reading them, her foot started tapping.

"What are these?" His eyes glanced up from the scraps, his eyebrows lifting.

None of your business. "Nothing. Could I have my notebook back...please?" She forced a sweet note at the end and even managed a smile.

Smiling back, he shook his head and went back to reading. "Just worry about picking out your present," he said, waving her away.

Do not stab him. Turning, she scanned the shelves and snatched the first title that caught her eye. "There. All done. Can

I please have my notebook back now?"

He looked up from her writing and glanced at the book in her hand. "Fascinating choice."

What was so fascinating about choosing a classic like Gone with the Wind? She narrowed her gaze on him. "What do you mean?"

He shrugged. "Just find it funny that you'd choose a novel that takes place when I grew up, that's all."

Her jaw dropped. She'd never thought about how old Charlie really could be. He didn't look much older than herself. "It was an interesting period in history, I suppose."

He sneered at that. "Interesting isn't the choice of word I'd use to describe the experience."

Her stomach fluttered with renewed curiosity. A dozen questions flitted through her mind. She tilted her head to the side. "How would you describe it?"

She saw his jaw tick as his eyes stared off into an unseen past. "Complicated."

Rolling her eyes at his vague answer, she stepped away from him. It seemed they both had their fill of strolling down memory lane. "Well, I'd better get to bed. Busy night, you know."

He nodded and placed the scraps back into the notebook. He held it out for her, and she grabbed it, her fingers brushing against his at the exchange. Tingles ran up her arm and she shivered. She risked a glance at his face, finding him staring at her as she hurried out the door.

As she was calling herself all sorts of stupid, her eyes caught movement down the hallway. It was the master's whore sneaking into his room again. Her gut knotted as she caught sight of her mother's bracelet flashing just before she disappeared into Master's quarters.

CHAPTER
THREE

I'VE GOT A BAD FEELING ABOUT THIS, CHARLIE THOUGHT AS HE watched Nessie hurry away. Even with ill-fitting clothes, his gaze tracked the feminine sway of her hips.

He'd sensed her the moment she had gotten within a few yards of the study door. His whole body tensed, warming in response to her presence. He'd opened the door, jumping at the chance to talk to her. *And she can't get away from me fast enough.*

Charlie didn't blame her for her wariness around him. The other vampires gave her plenty of reasons to fear his kind. Jacques' brutal feeding earlier was a prime example. The longer he spent with her in the study, the more he wanted to bask in her company. Not to mention the effects she seemed to have on him. His temperature hiked up another few degrees, and her scent made his head spin. That one slight touch of her hand sent shivers through his rapidly-heating body. Keeping his composure had taken constant effort.

He had sought Paul out earlier as soon as he'd finished showering. Paul had beamed at him. "My baby turned eighteen at sundown. Guess you were right about me getting old, huh," he'd said, chuckling and rubbing his balding head.

Somehow, Charlie had returned on the very day that Nessie turned of age, now old enough to be a vampire's destined mate. *His* destined mate?

He cursed to himself as he made his way back to his room. What the hell was he supposed to do with a human? His plans didn't include a mate, destined or otherwise. And he'd be damned if he'd let centuries of hard work go to waste over the woman. Jacques de Portea deserved to die, and he was finally close enough to land a lethal blow to the powerful immortal that had taken everything from him.

Lancaster, 1867

"Something's out there," his mother whispered, her wide-eyed gaze landing on his father. He nodded, his focus somewhere outside the window as his eyes darted trying to see through the darkness. His father snatched his rifle from the corner of the room. "Get under the floorboards." "What's going on, Pop?" Charlie asked, trying to keep the screech from his voice and failing. He didn't want to get in the crawl space beneath the house.

"Just do as I say, son."

"C'mon. I'm a man now. I fought in the war, for Christ's sake!"

His father clenched his jaw as he gripped his rifle and glanced out the window again. "Barely fifteen. You had no business volunteering. You're lucky I wasn't here to tan your hide for even thinking it."

"You were fighting in the war, too!"

"Your job was to look after your mother, not abandon her! Boys have no business fighting wars."

Charlie sighed, his shoulders slumping.

"Now get under the damn floorboards, and keep your mouth shut. I don't care what you hear or see, you stay down there, and you stay quiet. Ya hear me?"

Charlie nodded, following his mother over to the trap door and dropping through the hole. Then, his mother shut the trap door, throwing the handwoven rug over it.

"What are you doing, woman? Get your ass down there with him!"

"Oh, I don't think so, John Matthews. I watched both of you run off to war and there wasn't a damn thing I could do about it."

"Mary..."

"Throw me the other rifle."

Silence stretched for what seemed like hours before it came. Whatever it was. The door flew from the hinges, and Charlie heard the blasts from his parents' rifles a moment later.

"Nice try, humans," a cold, sneering voice said. His mother's scream pierced the air, drowning out a nasty gurgling sound.

Charlie could hear his heart pounding in his ears as he pressed his palm over his mouth. He peered up through the floor, only to see something dripping through the cracks. Blood pooled next to him and his stomach clenched. He'd fought grown men in battle, but whatever this was. It was no man.

"You are a pretty one, aren't you? Too bad for you I haven't drank in days, and one coal miner isn't quite enough for me," came a snide voice in the darkness. Charlie caught a glimpse of the man for only a second, but it remained etched in his mind in perfect detail. Narrow face, pale skin, icy-gray eyes under dirty blonde hair *that fell to his shoulders. A monster hidden beneath the handsome features.*

His mother's scream cut off. More blood poured through the cracks. There was nowhere to escape as it ran down his face, mixing with the silent tears he couldn't hold back and soaking his clothes. Under his feet, the puddle of blood expanded. And he was left to crouch down, shaking in his parents' blood.

His plan was simple from that day on: get close enough to the monster to kill him. No matter what. And he'd spent his life doing just that. The numbing effects of transitioning to vampirism made the horrific acts required by his Maker easier with each passing day. Now, that terrified boy was nothing but a distant memory. He crawled into bed wondering how to keep this new "mate" of his from complicating his plans.

Charlie moaned, his eyes fluttering as a gentle touch brushed across his forehead. Still half-asleep, he opened his mouth, ready to call out her name. Like a love-sick idiot.

The hair brushing over his bare chest made him realize he sported a raging hard-on. He opened his eyes, wanting to see her face before he kissed her.

Black eyes met his, matched by the sleek, dark hair around her face.

He groaned and pulled the covers over his chest, pushing her hand away from his face. "What are you doing in here?"

Kat's red lips curved in a sly grin. "Jacques wanted me to tell you you're wanted in the study. But you were obviously dreaming about me and I didn't want to interrupt what looked to be a deliciously wet dream." She leaned down, planting her hands on his chest.

"Jacques wants me in the study? For what?" He turned his head, avoiding her kiss.

Kat rolled her eyes. "How should I know? Who cares?" She slid a hand beneath the covers, sliding it over his hips and heading for his deflating manhood.

He shoved her off the bed. "Not now, Kat. I've gotta go see what he wants."

"Oh, come on. It'll only take a few minutes." She popped back up on her feet and walked around the bed as he rolled out on the other side and headed for the bathroom.

"I said, not now." He slammed the bathroom door in her pouty face.

He heard her growl loudly, his mattress squeaking as she hopped onto it. He showered and dressed in a hurry not wanting to keep Jacques waiting. The fashion of the area still resembled that of the late twentieth century. Though, unlike the previous century, the dark denim that now hugged his lower half was considered a luxury item. It took manpower (and, by that, he meant slave-power) to produce the fabric and then turn it into a wearable pair of pants. Only those of decent means could afford such an item. Slaves and the poorest of his kind typically wore whatever they could get their hands on to sew into their own clothes. Discarded bed sheets or blankets were common. In fact, he knew Nessie and the other slaves all wore such items. A twinge of guilt passed over him as he slipped the black cotton tee, another luxury item, over his head. He shook the all-too familiar feeling off and opened the bathroom door.

Kat lay naked on his bed, her head resting in her palm as she smiled at him, crooking her finger.

He shook his head and walked past her. "You're relentless." Grabbing a pair of socks from a drawer, he plopped down on the corner chair and slipped them and his boots on.

She crawled to the edge of the bed. "You like that about me."

Did he? Or had she just been an easy target? Even vampires had needs...

He shrugged, standing and leaving the room. Her shocked face made him snicker as the door shut.

Stepping into the study, he saw Jacques mutter something to Bobby, another slave, who bowed and dashed from the room.

He put on his best "at your service" face and stepped towards his Maker. "You summoned me, sir?"

"Ah, yes." Jacques' grin made Charlie's stomach turn. He recognized the evil spark in his Maker's pale eyes. "I wanted to remind you how slaves are dealt with. I think those old windbags at council softened you up a bit. And we can't have that."

Charlie blinked before straightening his face. "I apologize for disappointing you, sir."

"What did I tell you about apologizing?" Jacques studied him for a moment before smiling again. "Not to worry. We'll straighten you back out in no time."

"I look forward to it, sir." Already, his chest clenched at the prospect of what Jacques had in mind.

A moment later, his heart fell into his stomach as Bobby returned. Nessie followed him in.

Jacques moved and Charlie noticed him grab something off the shelf. He almost gasped as he saw what Jacques held. A book. *Gone with the Wind.*

He cursed himself to hell and back. How had he been so fucking stupid? His eyes darted to Nessie, who stood gazing back at him with those big, innocent eyes. He'd been so eager to please her, he'd done something he should've known not to. And now, Nessie would pay for his mistake. Because there was no way he could alert Jacques to her connection to him. She'd only suffer more. His eyes locked onto Nessie's face for a moment before he looked away. Gods, he deserved to rot in hell for this.

The smile plastered on Master's face made Nessie want to back away. But she didn't.

"Ah, there's our little thief." He stepped closer. *Don't move. Don't move.* Her eyes darted to Charlie, who seemed a little too interested in the wallpaper.

Master walked over to her, sneering. "I do not tolerate thievery of my property from my property."

Staring at him, she wanted to ask what the hell he was talking about. She knew better, though. Smart-asses weren't tolerated either. Instead, she glanced at Charlie again, hoping he'd clue her in.

Rough fingers grabbed her jaw, forcing her eyes back to Master's face. "Stop looking at him!"

She pressed her lips together as her jaw started bruising. His pale, beady eyes narrowed, his thin lips twitching.

"You will be punished for your thievery, girl," Master said, raising his hand and shaking the book at her. Her book. The one Charlie had given her as a gift the night before. "Take her to the courtyard, Charlie."

Her knees went weak and wobbly. The courtyard. She couldn't breathe. Her gaze landed on Charlie again. "You set me up, you bastard!"

Charlie's jaw ticked before he stepped from the bookcase. All calm and casual. "Sir, is this really necessary?"

Master jerked his head around, his eyes wide. "Of course, it's necessary! This slave," he spat, forcing her to look at Charlie now, "had the gall to think she was entitled to claim a book as her own. She is a slave! She doesn't have the right to claim shit!"

"Yes, but—" Charlie started, his eyes darting back to her.

"She is plenty old enough to know her place. To understand

the rules. Those who break the rules deserve to be punished." Master released her and got in Charlie's face. "Don't you agree?"

Charlie's eyes blazed fury as he offered a barely discernible nod of his head.

Master turned to face her, his gaze above her. "Take her to the courtyard. And bring Katherine and Logan in here."

Glancing behind her, she saw Bobby nodding his head before giving her a look of pity. He took hold of her arm and pulled her from the room.

CHAPTER FOUR

NESSIE SAT ON A SMALL BENCH IN THE CENTER OF THE courtyard. She tried not to tremble, but, as the other slaves began circling around her, her body shook and her cheeks flushed. She kept her eyes on her shaking hands, knowing what was coming, and knowing she had done nothing to deserve it.

Master finally stepped into the courtyard, a small grin on his face. Her body shook harder as she watched him come toward her.

"I am going to enjoy this," Master whispered to her as he

passed the bench.

You would you sick bas—. Her stomach clenched as she saw Charlie stepping into the courtyard with Katherine and Logan following close behind. So, he'd decided this little show was too good to miss? What a fool she'd been, calling him her friend. Well, she wasn't a naive little girl anymore, was she? Now, she saw him for what he truly was.

Someone grabbed her arms from behind, forcing her off the bench. Bobby pushed her chest against the column, making her wrap her arms around it and tying her wrists with a thick piece of rope.

Logan nudged Charlie forward, muttering something to him. He clenched his fists, his face twitching as he moved to sit on the bench she was just pulled off. Front row seat, even. How classy.

"This slave has been caught with this," Master began, holding the book up, "in her room. A book from my study." He threw the book at her feet. "Thievery will, in no way, be tolerated in my household." He turned toward her and nodded.

She sucked in a breath as the first lash ripped through the thin material of her shirt. In the short relapse, she scanned the crowd, finding her parents pushing through to the front. Her mother had tears streaming down her face, and her father threw a deadly gaze Master's way.

She hugged the column tightly as the next few lashes came down. Her back stung as if a whole nest of wasps had jabbed into her. And Master watched with a smile. She stared at him, not bothering to hide her hatred for the man responsible for her fate. He met her gaze, his grin fading with each blow that failed to draw tears.

"Harder," he directed whoever was delivering the whipping.

Each lash drew more blood from her battered body as she clenched her teeth so hard her jaw felt like it would explode. The vampires' gazes turned red with thirst, some of them revealing lengthening incisors. That scared her a hell of a lot more than any whip could. She prayed Master wouldn't allow them to feast on the blood that poured from her back afterward, shuddering at the thought.

Master's lip raised in a sneer that told Nessie he mistook her trembling as a sign the whipping was finally getting to her. She snapped her gaze back to him, glaring her hatred, making sure he saw there were no tears in her eyes. Even though her body wept with agony.

His nose twitched as he saw her determination, her refusal to show him the pain she felt with each crack of the whip upon her raw flesh. Then, he scowled and stepped forward.

"Give me that," he snapped, snatching the whip from Bobby's hand and shoving him out of the way. "I will break you, slave."

With Master behind her, her gaze fell on Charlie's face. Something was off. His eyes weren't glazed red like the others. His clenched fists shook at his sides, and he had murder in his eyes. Maybe, her murder. Then, why were his eyes still that vibrant blue?

She gasped, catching a scream in her throat as the whip tore through another layer of flesh. Her body clenched, and she finally shut her eyes, knowing if she didn't, the tears would stream down her face. Master gave her no time for recovery, the lashes becoming almost continuous.

"NO!" she heard Charlie and her father bellow together. She opened her eyes long enough to witness Charlie being held down by Katherine and Logan, struggling to get to her. Her father fought as Bobby and two more slaves dragged him from the courtyard.

"That son of a bitch! I'll kill him for this," her father roared as he was hauled away.

Charlie's gaze found hers in his bid for release, a single tear sliding down his pale cheek. Her jaw went slack for a moment. Vampires were capable of tears?

Her line of thought ceased as another blow rendered havoc on her broken body. All she could do was close her eyes and pray she would pass out.

"Jack." It was her mother. "Please. She's had enough."

Master growled. "She's had enough when I say she's had enough." As he continued to lash through her, it seemed he'd never be satisfied.

But finally, the blows stopped, and her body slumped against the column, even that tiny movement sending waves of sharp pain through her. Master glared down at her, and she had just enough strength to lift her head and open her tearless eyes.

Master's lip twitched again as his cold gaze narrowed on her. "Take her to Lockdown." He turned on his heel, dragging her mother behind him as he left the courtyard.

She finally let her head fall forward as the darkness took her.

Charlie yanked his arm from Logan's grip as they reached the door of his room. He had every intention of slamming the prick in the face, but he clenched his fist and exercised some control. Punching Logan would accomplish nothing but put Jacques on alert.

If Jacques wasn't *already* on alert. In a sick way, he hoped Jacques had been too focused on inflicting pain than noticing Charlie's reaction. Giving her a book was beyond moronic. He knew full-well how strict Jacques was with his slaves. But he'd had this overwhelming desire to please her and hadn't even thought of the dire consequences.

And getting upset over a simple whipping? He cursed himself. He knew better, but her pain had clawed at him. Even though his ass had remained firmly planted on that bench thanks to Kat and Logan holding him down. He tried to convince himself that the punishment didn't matter. Her pain didn't matter. *She* didn't matter.

But when Jacques had taken the whip himself, something had snapped inside him. He had to save her, to stop her suffering. No matter the cost.

Thankfully, Logan and Kat had been able to hold him back. Gods, why now? Why had Fate chosen now for him to find his mate? This uncontrollable connection with her could ruin everything.

Despite the giant wrench his new mate had thrown into his plans, there was no way he could reveal Nessie's connection to him to Jacques. He held mates to the same standard as all the vampires he sired. Which meant painful torture before death and transition. Charlie had yet to see a single vampire keep a mate under Jacques' rule. It always ended with both mates losing a head...or worse. Charlie knew it was because Jacques demanded complete loyalty. And a vampire would always, always choose his mate over his Maker. Every. Damn. Time. That was a big fucking wrench.

He ground his teeth and glared at Logan as he stood waiting for Charlie to open the door and retreat to his own room. He slammed through the door and turned to slam the door in Logan's face, but Kat had decided to come join them. Fucking joy.

Her bright red lips curved into a sly smile as she smacked her open palm on the door, holding it open. "I never would've pegged you for being soft about punishments," she chirped as she forced herself past Charlie and into his room.

He moved away from the door as Logan followed Kat, who had settled on his bed as if she belonged there. Her big, fake lashes batted at him as she patted the quilt next to her. He gave her a droll look and remained standing. With amusement still shining from her dark amethyst eyes, she teased him. "Aww, are you upset that we scratched up the little girl?"

He snorted. Little girl? Nessie had just won a battle of wills against Jacques. Which was a fucking disaster for him, but he had to admire her fortitude. He drilled his gaze into her. "Oh, I think we both can see she's not a little girl anymore, Kat."

Kat rolled her eyes at him. "She still follows you around like a little puppy like always," she said, her nails digging into the quilt. "She used to come looking for you in my room when we were..." Her lips curved into a sly smile. "Busy, remember?"

She looked up at him through her thick lashes as she slithered off the bed and sauntered over to him. Logan scowled at her as she slid her red, painted claws over Charlie's chest. "I'll come back later to jog your memory," she whispered as she stepped around him toward the open doorway.

"What?" Logan's angry glare passed over Charlie. "You will not come back later!" He roared as he followed Kat out of the room. Charlie snickered. Now he knew who had been tending to Kat's needs while he'd been away.

Kat snorted. "Oh, really? Who's gonna stop me? You?" She jabbed a finger into Logan's chest and laughed. Glancing back at Charlie, she blew him a kiss just before he slammed the door shut on the crazy bitch.

CHAPTER FIVE

NESSIE REMAINED IN LOCKDOWN FOR THREE DAYS. AND her bracelet didn't buzz one single time. She felt surprisingly good considering the beating she'd received. Apparently, the peace and quiet of the stone-walled cell had worked its magic on her body. And probably not having blood drained from her everyday helped, too. Too bad she couldn't think of a less painful way to get thrown into the damp, windowless cell.

"You look well."

She jumped, turning to catch Charlie watching her from the

doorway.

"Surprising. Considering I just got flayed open because of you," she spat at him. His face fell and she wanted to be glad to see his guilt. Instead, her chest ached at the reminder of another sharp blade of his betrayal. Then, she noticed the clothes in his hands. "Those for me?"

He snapped out of wherever his head had just taken him. "Yeah. Here." He held the clothes out for her.

She walked over to him, snatching the clothes from his hands and clenching her jaw at the zing that ran up her arm at the brief contact. His eyebrows puckered as he gazed down at her, sadness swirling in their blue depths.

She turned her back on him. As she swapped clothes, a smile broke across her face. Her back barely tingled as she stretched her arms overhead and pulled the clean shirt on.

When she turned, Charlie was staring at her, his eyes narrowing. He tilted his head. "How did you heal so quickly?"

Nessie crossed her arms over her chest. "Well, I did get to keep all of my own blood for a few days. Maybe that helped."

He raised his brow, shrugging before he turned to leave. She followed him upstairs, and he left her at the kitchen, disappearing down the hallway toward the East Wing. She stepped into the kitchen, where her mother bombarded her with a tight embrace. "Mom, my back," she groaned, feigning pain to get the wench off her.

"Oh, I'm sorry, dear," she sputtered, quickly releasing her and patting her cheek before returning to the whistling kettle.

Nessie looked around the large kitchen, frowning. "Where's Dad?"

"I haven't seen him since this morning."

She quirked a brow. That was unusual. Her father always made sure to greet her at sunset before they were required to begin their daily duties.

Her mother set a steaming cup in front of her. Nessie wrinkled her nose like she always did. Her mother glared, pointing down at the mug like she always did. Nessie debated telling her mother to shove that mug where the sun ---

A scream pierced the quiet kitchen, and all thoughts of tea were forgotten. Nessie was the first to run into Missy, one of the other house slaves. Her innocent thirteen-year-old face was horror stricken. She was running from the East Wing feeding room. Nessie caught sight of Charlie coming from the feeding room too. The girl's wide, brown eyes found hers. Tears streamed down her face as she took Nessie's hands.

"I'm so sorry. There was nothing I could do," she stammered between inhales, her body heaving as her hands shook. Nessie glanced up, catching Charlie's deep frown and wrinkled forehead. She tensed at the sight.

Nessie felt her mother brush past her, and when her mother's shriek rattled her ears, she rushed to follow her. Charlie stopped her before she could get near the doorway. She stared up at him, her eyes narrowing as he stood blocking the doorway.

"What happened?" she growled. Charlie's sad eyes studied her face before he sighed, stepping out of the way.

Nessie struggled to breathe. *Oh, gods, no. Please no.*

Her mother had collapsed onto the floor, sobbing into her palms. Blood splattered across the white furniture and walls, pooling on the floor in front of the sofa. There her father lay, motionless. She knew he was dead before her knees crashed beside him. Cradling his nearly-detached head in her lap, she tried not to vomit. Blood still leaked from the gaping hole in his throat, his eyes open and empty. No sparkle of affection when he looked at her. No glint of amusement at his own humor. Just...nothing. He was gone.

"Get this cleaned up."

Her gaze lifted as she felt the tears threatening to spill from her eyes. Master came through the doorway that led to the attached washroom, wiping his hands on a red-stained rag. Her blood boiled as a wave of rage swept over her, her vision zoning in on him. He took her father from her.

"You killed him!" Her body crashed into his, taking both of them to the ground. She hadn't planned on attacking him. Gods knew it was probably the dumbest thing she'd ever done. But in that moment, with her father's dead body behind her and the tears streaming from her eyes, she didn't care. A hot, red blanket of rage had descended upon her and she could do nothing but obey its violent call. *Kill him.*

Master's face contorted in shock and rage as he slammed against the floor, the rug beneath them sliding across the room. She raised her arms, but before she could bring her fists down on his ugly mug, someone snatched her off him. Throwing her body into a violent fit to get loose, she yelled, "You killed him, you bastard!"

Master got to his feet, brushing himself off as if she were dirty. "You will regret this defiance, girl," Master growled as he got in her face.

She stopped her struggling as she snarled at him. "Regret this, you piece of shit." She smashed her foot into his groin, drawing a howl from him.

"Take her back to Lockdown, now!" Master yelled, his eyes flashing death at her. She had probably signed her own death certificate with that low blow, but she didn't care. She was done caring.

It was Charlie that dragged her from the room as her mother watched, hovering over her dead husband's body, her face drenched in tears. She didn't utter a word. Doing nothing to stop the fact that her own daughter was being hauled away, most likely to await death.

"I hate you!" Nessie screamed as Charlie tore her from the room.

Shit, shit, shit. Charlie paced his room as he waited for dusk to fall. Nessie was a dead woman. No way would Jacques allow her to live after that foolhardy stunt. What was she thinking? Attacking a vampire was dumb to begin with. Attacking a vampire like Jacques was suicide. He shouldn't care. Really. He'd seen Jacques murder innocents before, right? Why should she be any different? She didn't matter to him anyway. She didn't fucking matter.

Jacques' furious bellow had Charlie dashing out the door and down the hallway. Peeking around the corner, he saw Nessie's mother, Eva, curled on the floor in front of Jacques' bedroom door, her face buried in her arms.

"What is wrong with your family? First, your decrepit husband threatens me, and then your defiant child attacks me. Me! Her fucking Master! You're lucky I'm not adding your head to a pike alongside them." Jacques' face flushed red with fury. "But you are mine, woman!" He kicked Eva in the stomach, making her grunt and groan. "Mine!" He crouched, yanking Eva's head up by her hair. Streaks of tears and blood covered her usually-beautiful face. "I refuse to allow your family to ruin my reputation. Slaves do not threaten and attack their masters. She will join her father at dusk."

Eva choked on a sob as Jacques threw her back to the floor. "No, please. Please, Jack." She tried to crawl after him, but each time she moved, she clutched her stomach. Jacques sneered at her before turning, the heel of his boots clicking down the stone floor as he stomped away.

Son of a bitch. Charlie hurried to her side when he was sure Jacques wouldn't return for another go at the poor woman. She gasped, her head snapping around to him. "What do you want?"

Vengeance, he thought, crouching down next to her. "Your daughter needs to be dealt with."

"No! No, please don't kill her!"

"Shhh! He'll hear you. Is everyone in your family stupid?!" he snapped.

She clamped her lips shut. First smart thing he'd seen all day.

"Good. Now, listen carefully. I cannot believe I'm saying this, but I can't let Nessie die." Just the thought of it made his chest feel like it would shatter into oblivion. "So, if you want her to live, you'll do as I say, understood?"

Eva gave a stiff nod, wincing. He held his hand out to help her to her feet, and he led her to her room before continuing.

"I know Jacques has a certain...interest in you." Eva pursed her lips. "I am going to need you to keep him, um, entertained until dawn."

Eva's eyes widened. "I'm not exactly his favorite person right now."

"Do you want your daughter to live or die?"

She snapped her mouth shut, bowing her head.

"Just answer the question."

"Fine. I'll do it. But why until dawn?"

"After dawn, he'll be stuck inside the mansion until sunset. But the longer you can keep him occupied, the better chance we'll have."

"Okay, but I don't know how -"

"I don't care how, just figure it out so I can get your daughter out of here with her head still attached."

He didn't wait for her to respond, leaving her to tend her wounds and figure out her battle plan on her own. He had his own plans to re-evaluate thanks to a defiant woman he couldn't keep himself from.

"Hey there, lover boy."

You have got to be fucking kidding me. Kat waltzed down the hallway in a red teddy that left nothing to the imagination. "Hope you're all rested up," she purred, wiggling her eyebrows.

He sighed. "I'm not in the mood, Kat."

Slamming her hands on her hips, she scowled. "Why are you avoiding me?" Her face softened and her purple hues shimmered at him. "I know it's been years, but I...I waited for you."

He snorted. "Yeah. Right. Logan doesn't seem to have gotten that memo."

"Logan? Who the hell cares about Logan?"

"Don't you?"

"Of course not! I'm with you."

"You haven't been with me in ten years. So, stop playing the desperate, lonely girlfriend card. It's pathetic."

"What the hell has gotten into you? This is about that little human girl, isn't it? You don't think I noticed how you used to dote on her all those years ago? Oh, and now she's all grown up and you don't need me anymore, is that it?"

He clenched his jaw stopping himself from telling her the truth. "Jacques can do whatever he likes to his slaves, including Nessie. I just need some time to adjust."

"Those ancients at council really did a number on you." She placed a hand over his heart and gave him a pitiful look.

"Yeah, they did. So, it's best you go to Logan for those needs."

She gasped and dropped her hand. "You want me to go to another man?"

"C'mon, Kat. We both know you're not picky. As long as he's willing, you're willing."

CRACK! Her hand slammed across his cheek before she turned on her heel.

He sighed as he watched her strut away with her nose in the air, hoping his unkind words did the trick. She needed to move on from him, if it was true she hadn't done so already. Which he still found hard to believe.

Once inside his bedroom, he slammed some essentials into a backpack in a hurry and caught sight of his bloodied cheek in the bathroom mirror. It seemed he couldn't get away from the damn stuff today.

CHAPTER SIX

NESSIE CLUTCHED HER STOMACH AS IT growled...again. *Shut it, you.* She didn't care about food at the moment. Even though she hadn't eaten since receiving her birthday gift. How she wasn't sprawled out on the floor, weak and moaning in pain, she had no idea. Perhaps Master planned on starving her to death. That would be a kindness uncharacteristic of his reputation. He certainly hadn't been that kind to her father.

Her eyes were finally dry. Red, and puffy as hell, but dry. She had no tears left. Depleting years' worth in a single night should have exhausted her. Must be the aura of inevitable death surrounding her that kept her from passing out in a heap of grief.

Her gaze darted to the door as she heard footsteps approaching her cell. Her heart raced at the sound, and her palms grew slick with sweat. The lock clicked open just before a dark head of hair popped through the opening.

Her fear evaporated. Master wouldn't delegate her execution. No, he'd want to experience it firsthand, up close and personal. Sick bastard.

"Get out," she snapped. Charlie was the last person she wanted to see. Well, almost.

"Now is that any way to talk to your rescuer?" He pushed the door wide open, leaning against it with his arms and legs crossed.

Now, he was just being a prick. No way was a vampire coming to her rescue. "Do I look like an idiot?"

"Not particularly, but you can prove me wrong later." He pushed off the doorframe and walked towards her. She backed up, matching him step for step until her ass flattened against the cement wall behind her.

He went to grab her arm, but she pulled it away. "Don't touch me."

"Then follow me." His face got within inches of her own. Waaay too close for comfort and he had her backed into a wall. Not good. Her body trembled, her heart thrumming in her ears.

"Why would I do that?"

He rolled his eyes, sighing. "We don't have time for twenty questions. Either follow me, or I'll carry your ass out. Pick one." His face pressed forward another inch. "Quickly."

She stood there speechless and lost in the mesmerizing swirl of silver in his stormy blue eyes. Whoa, what the hell? Mesmerizing? Where the hell did that come from?

She shook herself and clenched her teeth, her palms sweaty

again. This was not good. Because what choice did she have really? Stay here and die or...what? Charlie was the only alternative. And honestly, choosing between Master and Charlie. No brainer. Maybe Charlie would at least kill her quickly out of mercy. He at least *pretended* to be her friend all those years ago. More than she could say for any other bloodsucker around here. "Fine," she ground out. "Lead the way."

He nodded and gave her a quick smile. "Smart choice. Guess you're not an idiot after all." He backed away, letting her breathe again.

Smart ass. Pushing off the wall, she followed his backside, which wasn't a bad view, actually. She mentally smacked herself. *He could be leading you to your death. Stop admiring his ass.* Apparently, she was an idiot.

Charlie led her through dark, winding tunnels that ran beneath the extravagant mansion. "How long have these been here?" Nessie asked as Charlie led her to a small door.

"They were part of the Underground Railroad," Charlie said as he pushed the door open. Moonlight trickled through, casting an eerie glow over Charlie's face. Those mesmerizing eyes practically sparkled. "Now, stop ogling me, and let's go," he said with a huge smirk on his face.

She cleared her throat. "I wasn't ogling. I was hesitating," she insisted, sticking her chin in the air as she passed him and exited the tunnel.

She heard him chuckle behind her. "If you say so."

Moments later, she stood in front of a fresh heap of dirt.

His brows furrowed as he gazed down at the ground. "I thought you'd want to say goodbye to your father before we left." There was a crack in his voice that almost made her think vampires were capable of emotion. "I'm sorry, but you won't be able to see your mother."

Her chest tightened at his words. "What do you mean? Isn't

she coming?"

He pressed his lips together as he shook his head. "She had to stay behind to make sure we had a shot."

Her eyes stung as she gulped a lump her throat and looked down at the small heap of dirt. By month's end, the grass and weeds would overtake it, blending it with the rest of the large garden. At least they had given her father a beautiful place to rest.

Kneeling, she ran her fingers through the loose soil, feeling tears threatening to spill free. Her father deserved her tears. Deserved to see her sadness. Her grief at his absence. But her gaze darted up.

Charlie stood keeping watch, scanning the area, and she didn't want him to see her cry. No weakness. Crying would have to wait.

I'll miss you, Dad. She stood and turned towards Charlie.

"Ready?" he asked.

She nodded. "But I'm going alone." He'd broken her out of the cell and gotten her outside. Rescue complete. Mission accomplished.

Charlie stared at her for a moment. "Excuse me?"

"You heard me. I don't trust you."

He didn't blink, barely reacted at all. "I know."

"Why would I leave with someone I don't trust...at all?"

He leaned his face down, crowding her again, but, this time, she refused to step back. His eyes stared into hers and she had to swallow as her throat suddenly became dry. "Because you don't have any other option."

She scowled and looked away, letting the truth of his words sink in. Escape was unheard of. No one had ever accomplished it in her lifetime. And those who tried, had done so alone. And they had suffered alone. Master personally tortured them until they begged for death.

And she knew that because Bobby's wife had tried to escape years ago. Not long after Charlie had left. At dawn, she ran. At dusk, she was caught. Every slave in the mansion was forced to watch her torture. She was eventually bled dry. It looked like a slow, painful death: a specialty of Master's. Nessie wouldn't be surprised if that were to be her fate had Charlie not come to rescue her. Her eyes found his again. Well, he hadn't killed her yet, had he?

She sighed, defeated. She would have to put her life in the hands of a vampire.

Charlie smiled. "You're a fighter, Nessie. That's one of the reasons I think this might actually work." He had seen the truth of her resilience when Jacques had taken the whip to her. Not one tear. Even though he could see the agonizing pain written on her face. It had taken everything he had not to tackle Jacques to the ground to end her suffering. But then, they'd probably both be dead.

"Don't be a suck-up..." Pausing, she stared at him a moment before she pressed her lips together to keep from smiling.

He rolled his eyes. *Really*? "Yes, yes. Vampire. Suck up. You're hilarious. Let's go."

She gave him a curt nod and followed him toward the gate.

"I didn't realize it would be so easy," she whispered. "There are no guards or...anyone, for that matter."

Jacques was too arrogant to believe he needed guards to control his slaves. No, his reputation was usually enough to keep them in line. Especially with his high-tech control devices. "This is where it gets messy."

"Messy?" She stepped away from him.

He reached for her arm, but, again, she snatched it out of

reach. He sighed. *She hates you, remember?* "Your bracelet has to come off now. The GPS tracker inside will lead him right to us."

Her round eyes widened, the moonlight shining off the gold specks in her hazel irises. She knew the wires were embedded in the thin flesh of her wrist. Glancing down at the bracelet, she took a deep breath before nodding. She held her arm out, reminding him of the way she'd offered her wrist during their first feeding. That moment would forever be etched into his mind. It was the reason they were here, wasn't it? Her blood had broken the numbness. His emotions no longer muted, but a tidal wave crashing down on him. The memory of their friendship once felt like an old black and white movie he could watch but never feel. Now, he felt it in full technicolor. It made him crave her. Her scent. Her voice. Her blood. Her body. Her blood seemed to have awakened his very soul. Because he could no longer sit idly by and allow Jacques to kill her, as he'd done to so many innocents before her. Like her father. Like his own parents.

As soon as his fingers brushed against her skin, she gasped, her hand jerking away. Shock and confusion played across her face as she eyed him warily. *She feels it, too.*

If she was his destined mate, and each moment was only convincing him, then only her blood would strengthen him from now on. No other would do. The fact that he'd been repulsed by Kat was yet another sign. He'd need to feed from her every few days or he'd weaken. And he couldn't afford for that to happen if he wanted to take on Jacques. The escape would draw his Maker out, alienating him from his lackeys. That was step one of the new plan.

He cleared his throat. "It's best I do this fast, and it is critical you do not scream." He could see she was still shaken from the touch, but she clenched her jaw and nodded. He grabbed her hand, and she inhaled sharply at the contact. *Definitely feels it.* "Squeeze my hand if it becomes too painful."

Her delicate throat moved as she gulped, and his body shivered in response. She took a shaky breath before closing her eyes and nodding. His fingers gripped the steel band and yanked.

Her mouth opened in a silent gasp as her wrist was torn open. The barbs that protruded from the bracelet ripped from her skin, blood oozing down her forearm. Her hand crushed Charlie's, her nails biting into his skin as she bit her lip wide open. Already her blood had his mind fogging.

A second after the bracelet was free, Charlie lifted her wrist to his mouth. Her blood a beacon to his starving senses.

She managed to pull her wrist free. "What are you doing?"

"Healing you." In a blur, he snatched it back.

She struggled until his mouth slid over the tender part of her wrist. She froze, and his ears picked up her frantic heartbeat as his tongue made quick work of her ravaged wrist. Her blood invaded his system, each drop strengthening him and his need for her.

CHAPTER SEVEN

NESSIE STOOD MOTIONLESS UNTIL CHARLIE FINALLY LIFTED his head. The holes in her wrist sealed shut. His eyes were closed, a drop of blood escaping his lips, and he was visibly shaking. "Are you okay?" she asked, astounded when she heard her voice sound so breathless.

His eyes blinked open, a deep, dark red, making her step back. They'd never been that color before. They were always either bright red (during feedings) or blue.

"Sorry." He turned his head away and wiped his mouth clean. When he glanced back at her, his gaze shot to her mouth. He tried to contain a smile and failed. "Your lip is bleeding. I should heal that up too." His finger grazed along her lips, catching a drop of blood and bringing it to his tongue. And now, her mouth was tingling. What the hell was going on?

"No." She pushed a palm against his *very solid* chest. "You've helped enough, really." He chuckled as she took a step back and glared at him.

She dropped her hand, shuffling her feet as she fought to get her fluttering stomach under control.

"Feeling okay, Nessie?" Amusement dripped from his lush lips. *Good gods, he just licked your blood off those lips! Quit it!*

She crossed her arms over her chest, shrugging. "I'm fine."

"Your heart's racing awfully fast for you to be fine."

Damn his vampire hearing! "I just got my wrist ripped open. Give me a break!"

"Oh, right," He mumbled and motioned her through the gate.

"So which way now?" Because, having never set foot off the mansion grounds in her life, she had no clue. Maybe it was a good thing he was here, after all. As long as he kept those fangs to himself.

A smile broke across his face again.

She quirked her eyebrow. "What are you smiling about?"

Without a word, he hoisted her into the air. His arms wrapped around her body as he nestled her against his chest.

"Wh-what the hell?" She wriggled in his grasp. "Put me down!"

"Can't." He started running.

"Bullshit you can't!"

"Nessie," he said, not even sounding a little out of breath. "We need to put as much distance between us and this place as possible."

She huffed. Apparently, even the fastest human on the estate was still too slow. As she watched the scenery blur by, she had to admit Charlie was faster. Even with her added weight. *Just because it's necessary doesn't mean I have to like it.* And she didn't. Really.

"So, where are we going?" she asked, trying to fill the awkward silence. She didn't know how much good it would do, though. Being carried by a superfast vampire you kinda used to have a crush on before you even knew what crushes were made it hard to *not* be awkward.

"North."

"North? That's all you're gonna give me?"

"I'm taking you to the free colonies. At the poles."

Her jaw fell. "Aren't they a jillion miles away?"

His chuckle turned into a bark of laughter. "I never said this was going to be easy. What did you expect? A quick jot across town and you'd be free?"

Well...not exactly. But the freaking North Pole. Her head fell back in exasperation. "I'm gonna be stuck with you for a jillion fucking miles, aren't I?"

His chest rumbled. "If you play your cards right..."

Charlie ran the entire night, and she almost got comfortable in his arms. Almost. When he finally stopped and set her on her feet, she quirked a brow at him. "What? Is it finally safe for me to walk on my own again?"

"It's almost daybreak."

"Oh." Well, that explained it. She glanced around, noticing the pink tinge in the eastern sky, trying to locate where Charlie was going to escape for the day.

He must have realized her train of thought. "A house just up the road."

Nodding, she followed him, watching a cute little house come into view. Blue with white shutters, like clouds. She didn't realize how much she missed the daylight until that moment. As a young child, before she was required to perform chores, she remembered playing out in the garden, feeling the warm rays of sunlight on her face.

She glanced at Charlie. "Do you ever miss it?" she asked.

He looked at her, confused. "Miss what?"

"The sun. The warmth. Don't you miss it?"

He lifted his brows in surprise. Yes, they hadn't exchanged small talk in a decade. She was surprised with herself right now. He glanced up at the coming horizon. "I miss it every day."

Her head tilted to the side. "Then why become a vampire?"

His face tightened instantly, the hard set of his jaw ticking. "What makes you think I chose to?"

She considered that a moment. "I don't know. You vampires all act so...superior. Like you're proud to be a---"

"Monster?"

She met his hard gaze. "Yes."

"We don't all choose our fate. When you live as long as I have, you come to accept it."

Staring longer than she should because she'd once again forgotten how old Charlie really was despite his youthful appearance, she finally shrugged and looked away. "So, whose house?"

"Friends of mine."

"Friends? As in?"

"Yes, they're vampires."

"Okay. How is this a good idea? I thought we were trying to get away from vampires?"

"Kinda hard for me given that I am one."

Her hands went to her hips. *Smart-ass.*

He shrugged and began walking toward the house, not bothering to see if she was following. *Arrogant smart-ass.*

She jogged to catch up as Charlie neared the steps of the small porch. What Charlie's plan was she had no idea, but she didn't want any more vampires knowing about her escape. Hell, she didn't want any more humans knowing about it.

Her eyes darted to a group of trees at the edge of the clearing the house sat in. She hesitated as her foot hovered over the bottom step. Dawn was close, but she could keep going. Even without---

His fingers wrapped around her wrist, and she snapped her head towards him, rearing back as her face almost smashed into Charlie's. His grip on her wrist tightened as he stopped her from falling on her ass.

He narrowed his eyes. "Don't even think about it."

She tried to pull out of his grip, but he wouldn't budge. At least he wasn't crushing her hand. She huffed, "I wasn't thinking about anything."

He shook his head. "Don't lie, Nessie."

"I'm not."

"Yes, you are. Stop. You suck at it."

She stuck her tongue out at him. Jerk. He shook his head again before pulling her up the stairs and tugging her toward him as he approached the door.

His fingers left her wrist only to slide down and twine with her own, tingles running up her arm and making her tremble.

He rubbed his thumb against her palm. Was he trying to comfort her?

She glanced at him as he tapped lightly on the door. Her face heated as he tugged her closer, her arm brushing against his.

He gaze flickered down to her, the corner of his lips lifting. "Are you blushing?" She would've smacked that smirk off his face if the door hadn't opened at that moment to reveal a pretty blonde woman.

She smiled at them. "Charlie. So nice to see you." Her eyes shifted to Nessie. "Who's your friend?"

Friend? They weren't friends. Anymore. Nessie tried to pull her hand out of Charlie's, but he held it tight. A smile planted firmly as he answered, "This is Nessie. We were wondering if we could inconvenience you for the day?"

The woman smiled warmly, exposing just a hint of fang. Nessie's fingers grasped Charlie's just a little tighter, and he squeezed back.

"Of course," she said in a sing-songy voice. She gestured them inside and Charlie gave Nessie's hand a little tug. She glared at the back of his head. *I'm not a ragdoll, asshole.*

A fireplace flickered in the corner of the small living room. A plush green rug with a huge purple flower lay on the hardwood floor. On the fireplace mantle were several frames holding pictures of what could only be perceived as a couple and their families. A large photo of the couple hung above the fireplace. The woman dressed in a beautiful white gown that faded elegantly to red at the hem, the man in a sharp gray suit.

Said man was lounging on a dark brown sofa as he watched a large hologram television displaying some kind of fighting match.

"Honey, we have company. Do you mind?" the woman chirped.

The man turned. "Oh. Hey, Charlie," he said, clicking a remote that made the hologram disappear. The two men shook hands just as the automatic shutters lowered, covering the windows and locking into place. They looked to be the same kind as the mansion's window shutters, specially designed to block out all sunlight.

Charlie pulled her toward him. "James, this is Nessie. She was one of Jacques' slaves."

James' gaze lowered to her. "Was?"

"We're running away," Charlie stated.

She whipped her head around. Why would he tell them that? *Charlie, you idiot!*

The woman clapped her hands excitedly. "Oh, my gosh. They're running away together. How romantic!"

Romantic? The woman could not be further from the

truth. This was Mission: Save Nessie's Ass. She glanced over at Charlie. Who was beaming down at her.

James chuckled. "Don't go all mushy already, Dina." But Dina was already flitting about, insisting on getting the guest room ready.

In no time, Dina showed Nessie to the guest room. And it was g-g-g-gorgeous with a capital G. A bed almost as large as Master's (she would know having had to make the stupid thing daily) was adorned in a floral quilt with ruffled pillows at the large, wooden headboard. Suddenly, Nessie felt exhausted despite having been carried all night. The lamps on each side matched the color of the flowers and cast the room in a cozy glow. Charlie swept into the room, depositing their very few belongings in a trunk at the foot of the bed.

He tilted his head towards her. "You can have first dibs on the shower," he said, taking a seat in the plush armchair in the corner of the room.

Nessie's mouth fell open. "Sh-shower? *I* can use the shower?"

A few minutes later Nessie moaned in absolute bliss as the warm jets of water relaxed all her tension from the hectic night away. Now she completely understood why the vampires of the house (especially the female ones) could spent an eternity in the shower. And why they each had their own bathroom. Slaves weren't permitted to use the showers. Unless you were sleeping with Master. Like her mother. Master didn't like his whores filthy like the rest of them, she supposed. The rest of them had to sponge bath or use the garden hose, which was a tad cold come winter.

She sighed as she rinsed her hair, knowing she couldn't stay in here forever. So, she forced herself to turn off the water and wrap an oh-so-soft towel around her body. She caught a blurry reflection of herself before glancing down at the items on the counter. Her heart skipped a little beat as she saw all the items she was never allowed to use. A hairbrush was the first thing she picked up, yanking the tangles out of her hair. And, after making her mouth minty fresh, she eyed the colorful powders and tubes of lipstick that lined the shelf.

A knock at the door had her jumping and grasping her towel. "You didn't drown in there, did you?" She could hear Charlie's amusement. Giving the makeup one last longing look, she turned towards the door. She didn't have a clue what to do with the stuff anyway.

Charlie allowed several seconds to tick by. "Nessie?" Nothing. Had she snuck out while he'd been talking to James? "Ness, this is not funny." Worry was creeping into his voice, and he tapped his foot as he waited for her to answer. If she'd run off and he had to hunt her down at sunset... An entire minute passed. "Vanessa, if you don't answer me, I will break down this door." Last chance.

A loud huff came from inside the bathroom before the door flew open. "I'm fine. It's a shower, not a swimming pool. Good grief, I'm not a toddler." Nessie stood in the doorway giving him a droll look. Her arms crossed tightly under her breasts, pushing them up in the most delectable way. *Don't stare.*

But seeing her in nothing but a towel almost knocked him right on his ass. He was once again reminded of the years that had passed in his absence. And the years had been kind to the scrawny little girl he'd once known. With the ill-fitting clothes of slavery gone, her curves were suddenly not-so-subtle. And his fingers itched to run over every single one of them. He clenched them and took a breath to calm himself. Instead, Nessie's scent filled his lungs, stealing his breath away. The layers of grime from Lockdown had been washed away and he caught the untainted scent of her for the first time. His fangs lengthened of their own accord in response.

He cursed, turning his head away and smashing a hand over his mouth. As if he needed another reason to want her.

"Are those clothes for me?" Nessie's voice chirped behind him, making him risk a peek. Her big, round eyes sparkled as she stared at the several outfits Dina had laid out for her to choose from. When her mouth opened, curving in delight, he took a step back to stop himself from taking her gorgeous mouth with his own. *It's the clothes making her smile, not you.* Damn, he wished *he* could make her face light up that way.

Clearing his throat, he stepped toward the door. "I'll leave you to dress, then."

He hurried out, finding Dina fluttering around the kitchen, fumbling with pots and pans. She turned to put a large pot on the stove, smiling that mega-watt smile she gave to everyone. "Did she like them?" she asked, hope shining from her baby blues.

He chuckled at her. "Well, from the drool dripping from her mouth..."

She squealed, her smile widening (if that was possible). "Oh, goody. I do hope they fit. Those rags Jacques made her wear did her no justice."

You're telling me. An image of Nessie in that scrap of a towel had him clenching his fists again. Though, he was glad Jacques had kept her beauty so well hidden. He'd seen mated males slaughter another just for staring too long. Hopefully, they didn't come across any other males, or he might be forced to pluck some eyeballs. Shit, this was bad. He had always had a nasty penchant for violence. Brawling in school, volunteering for war, developing an unhealthy obsession for vengeance. Now, being mated to a humble beauty that would undoubtedly draw the gazes of any free male. Fate just loved testing his limits, didn't she?

Dina's second squeal pulled him from his thoughts. "Oh, you look great in that!"

Charlie turned and felt his eyebrows raise in surprise. She'd chosen a pair of jeans that hugged every long inch of her legs, and a black sweater that fell off one shoulder, just begging for a slow caress down that smooth curve of her neck. With his fangs. Mouth. Hands. Shit, nothing! Nothing! *Get control of yourself.*

"Did you enjoy your shower?" Dina asked, beaming.

Nessie smiled back. "Immensely. Thank you."

"You should both get some rest," Dina said. "Charlie you can sleep on the couch. I'm sure Nessie needs that bed more than you do."

"Oh, that's not nec---" Nessie started.

"Works for me," Charlie said, winking over at Nessie. "Unless you wanted to share the bed..."

Nessie's mouth dropped open for a moment before she snapped it shut and shook her head. "Good night, then." She threw a quick smile at Dina and bolted for the guest room.

James slapped a hand on Charlie's shoulder, shaking his head. "Good luck with that." He thrust a blanket and pillow into Charlie's arms.

"Yeah, thanks." Charlie nodded to the couple before retreating to the living room for some much-needed sleep.

A loud ringing by his ear woke him a few hours later. He groaned and turned over, throwing the pillow hover his head.

"I got it," he heard James call. "Hello? Oh, Viktor. So nice to---oh, you're coming for a visit? Tonight?" James pitch raised. "No, no, we'd love to have you. Alright, I'll let Dina know. See you then."

James hung up the hologram and cursed.

Charlie sat up on the couch and gave a long sigh. "This isn't good."

A clang came from the kitchen and the two of them padded

over.

"Nessie?" Charlie blurted, tilting her head as he found her tip-toeing on a chair to reach a high shelf.

She gasped and tumbled from the chair. He dashed across the room, catching her just before her head smashed against the counter. Her cheeks flushed as she stared up at him and mumbled, "Thanks."

"What are you doing in here?" he asked.

She gave an uncomfortable shrug.

Dina slipped into the room, pecking James on the cheek. She glanced over at he and Nessie, her eyes widening. "Oh, you didn't have to put dishes away! You're a guest."

Charlie glanced down at Nessie, finding her cheeks reddening again.

"Dina, your father just called," James said. "He's coming for a visit tonight." They both frowned.

Dina pulled a pot out of the cupboard. "How long until sundown?"

James checked his watch. "About an hour."

"Fudge," she snapped. The closest she would ever get to an actual profanity. Bless her sweet heart. "This changes things." She caught Nessie off guard, squeezing her hand. "Nessie, I am so sorry about this."

Nessie raised an eyebrow. "I'm confused. What is so bad about your father coming?"

Dina sighed. "My father isn't quite as, ummm, sympathetic to the human plight as we are. He and Jacques are business partners. And if he realizes what you and Charlie are doing..."

Dina didn't need to finish. Charlie watched as Nessie's breath hitched, coming in shallow bursts. She pulled her hand from Dina's as she tried to retreat from the room. Turning to flee, her body smashed into his chest. He reached for her on instinct, the need to comfort her rushing through him.

"Don't touch me!" Tears welled in her eyes as she shoved his hands away. Her eyes darted around the room, landing on James, who blocked the other exit from the kitchen. He recognized the primal survival mode as she sought a way out. Panic setting in as each route was barred from her. She glared up at him as he touched her arm. Yanking it from his grasp, she reared back. He understood the need to pound something when anger-fueled adrenaline drove your actions. So, she might as well get it out and over with. Because he was *not* letting her get away. The blow to his cheekbone sent ripples of pain through his face, making him stumble. What the fuck was that? When he recovered a moment later, he spotted her tackling James to the ground. Successfully. What in the gods' names was going on here? His left cheek still throbbed as he ran after Nessie dashing for the front door. If she made it, she'd be gone. And he wouldn't be able to go after her in the daylight. Son of a bitch. What had Fate saddled him with?

When she reached her hand out to grab the doorknob, he made a leap for her. *Don't open the door, damn you!* He managed to snag her ankle. As her body made a nasty thud against the hardwood floor, he winced. Until her foot smashed into his bad cheek, making him call her a particularly nasty name.

"Holy shit, she's strong," James muttered as he grabbed her other ankle. "Are you sure she's human?"

"She smells human," Charlie replied as they both dragged her back and planted her on the sofa. His eyes found hers for a moment...so much contempt. But she settled down as she seemed to realize she'd lost the battle.

"You drank my blood, you moron. You know I'm human. Maybe you guys aren't as macho as you seem to think. Misogynistic assholes," she muttered as she averted her gaze and crossed her arms over her chest. "So, what? Am I a prisoner again?"

Charlie knelt in front of her, but she refused to look at him. "It would be foolish of you to run now with sunset less than an hour away. You know that, Ness."

She glared at him. "I'll take that as a yes."

Sighing, he dropped his head. "If it keeps you alive, then yes. I can't let him get you. He'll kill you. And this time he won't wait until dusk."

"So, what do I do then? Hide?"

Dina finally chimed in. "Unfortunately, it's not that easy. My father and I are quite old. We can smell you no matter where in the house you hide."

"So, what do I do?" Nessie repeated.

Dina paused, looking to Charlie for support. He let out a long breath, locking gazes with Nessie. "Act."

CHAPTER EIGHT

NESSIE STOOD IN FRONT OF THE BATHROOM MIRROR, bristling at the thought of the upcoming evening. Her clothes had been swapped out for another ill-fitting knee-length skirt and stained t-shirt that was once James'. She was a slave once more, at least for the night. She took deep breaths, trying to remind herself that if she played her part, she would never have to do this again.

The door opened behind her and Charlie walked in, dressed in one of James' casual suits. She turned to him, her hands going to her hips. "I'm never going to pull this off. We both know I can't act. Even when I was a slave, I played the part terribly."

The corner of Charlie's mouth kicked up in a small grin.

"See, you're trying not to smile because it's true." She turned back to the mirror, whipping her hair into a ponytail. But it still looked way too clean.

Charlie came up behind her, looking down at her through the mirror. "If you're trying to look less attractive, you are failing miserably."

Her eyes found his, and she saw her cheeks blush as she met his gaze. He found her attractive? She swallowed a mouthful of stutters before they could leave her mouth. *Nope, nope. Not going there.* She glanced in the mirror again and sighed. "I look way too clean to be a slave."

"Here, let me help," Charlie muttered, sliding his fingers through her hair. Tendrils of pleasure wove through her at the small touch, knotting her stomach and flushing her with heat. "There. Now, you at least look like you've done some work today rather than lounged around in the shower."

He winked at her, and she rolled her eyes at him, ignoring the tingles that his touch provoked. Dammit, what was wrong with her?

Glancing back in the mirror, she saw he had tousled her hair, making several pieces come loose and fall around her face.

He leaned down, his eyes hooded as he whispered in her ear, "Now, all we need to do is get you sweaty."

She gaped at him. Was he suggesting...? Clearing her throat, she muttered, "I'd better get out there and... fluff the pillows or something useless like that." Besides, she needed to get away from him before she did something stupid. Like enjoy his company. *You're not ten years old anymore, and you gave up on that crush a long time ago. When he left you. And didn't come back. Not like he can't easily disappear again. He's sure as shit fast enough.*

Charlie chuckled as he turned to the side to let her pass.

In the kitchen, Dina was a ragged mess. Nessie never thought a vampire could even be clumsy, but she was pulling it off brilliantly. She muttered to herself as she reached into a cupboard and lowered a stack of bowls onto the counter, making them clatter.

Catching sight of Nessie, she gave her a quick smile. "Oh, good. Nessie, could you grab some blood bags from the fridge and put them on the stove to heat?"

She paused for a moment. "Ummm, yeah, sure." She went to the fridge and grabbed a few bags full of blood from the shelves. That seemed to be all that the fridge contained anyway, so no way was she grabbing the wrong thing. Having had years of experience, she knew her way around the kitchen and soon had a pot on the stove. She held her breath as she squeezed the contents of each bag into the large pot and turned the stove on low.

She glanced over at Dina, who was still gathering utensils and some wine glasses. "Have to say, I've had a lot of experience cooking, but first time I've ever cooked blood before."

Dina looked at her, her eyes wide with shock a second before she tittered. "Oh, of course. I'm sorry. I can do that if you'd like." She moved to take Nessie's place.

Nessie put her hand up. "No, no. It's fine. I've had to deal with plenty of blood, too."

Dina's hand covered her mouth as her eyes turned sad. "Oh, my. I didn't even think of that. Really, I'm sincerely sorry."

Nessie smiled at her apology. For a vampire, she seemed very emotional. Odd. Nessie had always thought that vampires lacked emotions. Or at least had muted emotions. If not for the whole being a vampire thing, they might be friends.

She cleared her throat. "So, how exactly do you cook blood, anyway? Is it like soup? Do you have to stir it?"

Dina giggled. "No, not quite. Just keep on low. The goal is

to warm it to body temperature."

Her smile faded a bit as she was reminded that even a vampire as nice as Dina still drank human blood. She looked back down at the pot. "That makes sense."

"Well, if you think you can handle that, then I'm going to go set the table," Dina said and skipped out of the room.

A moment later, Dina returned with James pushing her back into the kitchen. "Have you lost it, Dina? It's HER job to set the table."

Nessie's jaw clenched as she realized he was talking about her. She glanced up at the couple, seeing James mouth an apology for his rudeness. Oh, right. She was playing slave for the night. Best hop to it then.

She grabbed the dishware from Dina and headed for the dining room.

Doing her best to keep her eyes averted, she entered the room where Charlie and a tall, thin man, whom she assumed must be Dina's father, sat. She remained silent, setting the table around them.

"So, this one's yours, Charlie?" Dina's father asked in a heavy Irish accent. Her body tensed, but she continued to work around them.

"Yes, this is her."

A hand grazed her rear, and the wine glass she grasped shattered. Her gaze darted to Charlie.

Charlie stood. "Viktor, I must insist you not touch her inappropriately. She is mine. I'm sure you understand." Her eyes widened in shock at his insinuation. If not for the creepy old bat trying to feel her up, she might have smacked him.

The hand left. "Of course." Viktor's goatee twitched, his lips curving. "I don't blame ye for that. For a human, she is an exquisite specimen."

"Nessie, get this cleaned up," Charlie commanded.

Nodding, she gathered the broken shards and hurried from the room before she broke something else. This might be harder than she thought.

To her surprise, the remainder of the evening passed relatively uneventful. She kept her mouth shut and did what she was told like a good little slave, and Viktor kept his grimy hands off her. Thanks to Charlie's claim on her. The fact that she was forced to rely on one man staking a claim on her to prevent another one from harassing her had her wanting to sock someone in the throat. Preferably a male someone. She almost wished she wasn't human so she could protect her own ass. Almost.

Instead, she gathered the dishes from the table, catching Charlie whispering to Dina. Dina blushed and turned to look at her. "Nessie, you can leave those in the sink and do them later. Charlie would like you to join him in his guest room while he, ummm, rests."

Viktor snickered as his dark, beady eyes roamed her body and a chill ran down her spine. She forced herself to keep her face neutral and nodded.

Charlie followed her into the kitchen. No sooner had she gotten the dishes into the sink when he took her hand, led her back through the dining room, and down the hallway before nudging her into the room and closing the door behind them.

She turned, her face coming just inches from Charlie's chest. She inhaled sharply and took a quick step back. His gaze bore into her as his finger came up to rest on his lips. Shhh...

Message received. She kept quiet as Charlie pointed to the bathroom door and allowed him to usher her into the bathroom, closing them inside.

He turned the shower on full-blast and smirked at her. "That should help convince them without having to act it out."

Her cheeks heated at the vivid picture his words evoked. And the bright fluorescent lights of the bathroom would do nothing to hide it. Charlie's mouth twitched its way into a full-blown smug son-of-a-bitch grin. No doubt he'd spotted her rosy cheeks. She crossed her arms and huffed. "Shut it, you."

He raised his arms in surrender. "I didn't say anything."

She turned to the mirror, yanking the band out of her hair and snatching up a brush. "Yeah, well, your face did all the talking."

She caught sight of him laughing in the corner of the mirror, and for a fleeting moment, he was knock-your-socks-off gorgeous. His face lit up all the way to his eyes, and she was reminded of the Charlie she knew as a child. The one she'd crushed on in the worst way. His eyes lifted and she knew he caught her staring at him. And for some unknown reason, she didn't look away. His laughter slowly faded as his gaze locked onto hers. His eyes shifted from their normal stormy blue to deep, dark gray until his pupils disappeared into blackness.

Turning from the mirror to face him, her gaze found his again. She tilted her head to the side. "I've never seen your eyes go black before." Her voice was little more than a whisper. She didn't want to risk any superhuman ears overhearing.

He nodded, slow and deliberate, his eyes roaming her face. He took a small step closer as his eyes returned to hers. "It's a vampire thing."

"Oh," she muttered simply because her mouth wouldn't form any other intelligent reply. Was it getting hot in this bathroom? Must be the steam from the shower.

Another step. She licked her suddenly dry lips, and his gaze darted to her mouth. The room heated another ten degrees as she tried to clear her throat and failed. "Ummm, what kind of vampire thing exactly?"

Her stomach knotted as he came within arm's length of her. He lifted his gaze to hers, his eyes seeming even blacker than before. "It's a sign of arousal."

The breath she hadn't realized she'd been holding rushed out as his words finally made sense of the strange sensations plaguing her since his return. She may be innocent, but she had read an entire library of books on almost every subject imaginable and the meaning of that simple word hit her like a ton of bricks. The room shrank as his black gaze drilled into her and he took another step.

She tried to back away, but her ass hit the counter's edge and she gripped it. Her breath caught in her throat. She was trapped. Stuck in this infernal bathroom with the very vampire who once drank from her wrist on the white sofa now stained with her father's blood. Stuck in this house full of the very creatures that robbed her of freedom, happiness, and the only person she had ever loved. Her breathing shifted, coming in short bursts as the panic sank in. She could try to make a run for it, but, in a house full of vampires, she wouldn't get far.

Suddenly, Charlie took several steps back, coming to rest on the opposite wall. She watched in silence as his eyes slowly regained their stormy blue color. "I'm sorry, Nessie," he whispered, his gaze shifting away as if ashamed. He looked at her again moments later, his eyes sad and full of regret. "I would never hurt you."

She stared at him, taking in his words, the sadness on his face, the regret so plainly written there. What he regretted, she wasn't sure. Revealing to her so openly his attraction to her? Having been one of her oppressors as a slave? The thought angered her. Anger at him for daring to be attracted to her. To think of her in the same disgusting way Master had used her mother. Anger at herself for being unable to control the physical reactions her body had to his presence. Her jaw clenched and she narrowed her gaze on him. "You did that the day you left ten years ago." His eyes widened before she turned away from him and resumed

brushing her hair, refusing to look at him.

CHAPTER
NINE

SEVERAL HOURS LATER, CHARLIE SAT IN THE CHAIR IN THE corner of the room pretending to read a book. He couldn't keep himself from glancing at Nessie as she tossed in the large bed. He'd, of course, had to argue with her about getting as much rest in the comfort of a proper bed as possible. The woman didn't know how to *not* argue with him. A huffy "fine" was the only word she'd spoken to him since being locked in the bathroom together.

He'd practically kicked himself in the mouth for what happened. Nessie wanted nothing to do with him. And now...well, now he knew why. He was her friend. And he left her.

Alone and unprotected in the service of a monster. But he'd had little choice. Jacques had told him to leave, so he did. Always the obedient servant in the eyes of his Maker. No matter the cost.

Philadelphia, 1872

This was it. No going back now.

"I do hope you don't disappoint me, boy," the monster muttered from behind him.

"I will not, Master," Charlie said, loud and clear for all to hear. He pressed his palms against the stone wall, gulping down a lump in his throat. Show no fear. "A painful death rears a stronger immortal, so I shall welcome the pain with open arms."

He heard grunts of approval from the others that had gathered for the ritual.

"That's my boy," Jacques praised, his sneering face coming into view. "Stay conscious for as long as you can. Only then will I decide if you are worthy."

Charlie nodded. "Of course, Master."

Jacques disappeared behind him again. A moment later, Charlie gritted his teeth as pain licked across his back. Fuck, that hurt. When the second lash came down, he hissed to keep from screaming. The third made him gasp. And the fourth almost buckled his knees.

He lifted his palms from the wall, ready to run from the agony that had just begun. The war was nothing compared to the cruelty of this monster. But as he turned his head, catching a glimpse of the arrogant smirk on Jacques' face, he stopped himself.

No. You will not give in. Push past the pain.

He set his jaw, planting his hands on the stone every bit as cold as his heart. Cold as the day that monster drained his parents dry and took all he had in the world.

The lashes came down harder, but he refused to close his eyes, scraping his palms on the ridged edges of the stones. He needed this. He had to prove himself worthy. Otherwise, the last five years would have been for naught.

Only after his back was raw and oozing buckets did the lashes end. He lifted his weary head to stare into the monster's eyes. And the crazy son of a bitch was beaming at him.

"You have the strength of one worthy of the gift." Jacques sliced his own wrist with the dagger and held it up for the crowd. "Tonight, we welcome a true warrior into our coven!"

The crowd cheered; a hazy roar heard through a mind fogged by pain.

"Drink, my son. And be reborn in a body worthy of your superiority."

Charlie didn't hesitate, opening his mouth to let the tainted blood drip onto his tongue, swallowing greedily. Jacques was pleased, which made his stomach clench, disgusted with himself.

The crowd settled down as Jacques stepped away from him. When the lashes began again, Charlie sighed. It was almost over now.

His heart, or what was left of it, ached at the thought of what he would become.

It's necessary, his mind argued, beating his heart into submission. To kill a monster...you must become a monster.

Yes, always the obedient servant...until he'd tasted a certain woman that kept rustling the sheets on the bed.

The clock on the bedside stand read 5:30 p.m. Dusk was an hour away, and he could tell from Nessie's breathing and heart rate that she hadn't slept a wink. Suddenly, she turned over, her bright eyes seeming to focus on him in the dark. After long moments of staring at each other, she narrowed her gaze. "Why did we have to stay in the bathroom so damn long?"

His eyebrows raised at the surprising question, and he

couldn't quite stop himself from smirking for a moment. He took a breath, straightening his face before responding. "Vampires are known for their...stamina."

He watched as comprehension broke across her face and she turned away, gazing at the ceiling. "Oh," she muttered and let out a long breath. "Well, that explains a boatload, doesn't it?" He heard her gag at the thought.

He snapped the book shut. Not being interested in a relationship with him was one thing... "Is it so horrid a thought you need to gag?"

She didn't bother looking at him as she shrugged. "I never understood why Mother had to stay in Master's bedroom for so long. She never came back until close to dusk most days. Now I know why." Then, she looked over at him. "And yeah, that particular thought makes me want to vomit."

"Ah, I see." So, it was Jacques she found repulsive, not *him*. What a relief. "Well, some humans find vampires very attractive," he coaxed.

Her eyes narrowed as she pursed her lips. "And some vampires take advantage of their slaves, who have no fucking say in the matter."

Okay, then. Not ready to own up to the attraction, obviously. He cleared his throat. "That's the unfortunate truth in some cases, but not all." He stuck his nose back into his book.

"I get why a vampire would be attracted to a human. Free blood source and all. But why would a human possibly want to be with a vampire?"

Charlie sighed, shaking his head. Her narrow-minded approach to the situation reinforced his fear that he'd never get her to accept him as a valid choice as a mate. Destined or not. And being a non-vampire, she had much less at stake by not accepting. This was more than an uphill battle. It was Mt. Fucking Everest.

He glanced up from his book to retort, his words catching in his throat. She'd rolled onto her stomach to face him, her waves of honey-colored hair falling over one shoulder, and the oversized collar of her sweater gaping open. Revealing the creamy mounds of perfection his mind had been imagining since the towel incident. Her breasts pressed into the mattress, hiding her nipples from sight. Dammit.

Her eyes turned wary, and he knew his had gone black again. Like he could help it with all that cleavage calling to him. "Nessie, your shirt." His voice croaked as he forced his eyes closed and worried his bottom lip with a fang. *Control. Get yourself under control.* And then, the unthinkable happened. The sweet scent of her body wafted over him, no doubt darkening his eyes further and making his entire body tense. He snapped his gaze back to her, where she stared at him with wide eyes and that pretty mouth open in surprise. Practically begging him to latch onto her lips and surprise her even more. Her skin was wondrously flushed as she sat with her sweater inching down her shoulder.

He bolted up from the chair as he struggled to keep control of his rising need. Too soon. Way too soon. Because she was not ready for what his body wanted to dish out. He shoved a hand through his hair, pacing, which only brought him closer to her. And all that heavenly goodness beckoning him to touch. Caress. Lick. Bite. "Sweet gods, Nessie. I can smell you from here."

He peeked at her, finding her tilting her head in confusion. Still looking good enough to eat. Literally. He had to get away from her before he did something unspeakable. Cursing, he darted into the bathroom and shut the door.

When he emerged thirty minutes later, Nessie was bundled inside the comforter, peeking out at him as he returned to the chair. He picked the book up to at least pretend to read again.

"What could you even smell? I just showered. I can't smell worse than I had this morning."

The woman just couldn't help herself. Too inquisitive for her own good. "I have a strong feeling you'd rather not know. You won't like the answer."

He heard her huff inside her bundle of blankets. Where she remained. For about thirty seconds. Too impatient for her own good, too. Throwing the blankets off her, she crossed her arms. "Tell me anyway."

Chuckling, he hid his face further inside the book. "Curiosity killed the cat, Vanessa."

He saw her bristle at the name, knowing she'd always hated it. He feared it was because her mother always called her by her full name. She'd always preferred her father's pet name.

"Good thing I'm not a cat then," she growled.

"If you insist," he sighed.

"I do insist."

He lowered the book, and there she was. Giving him that classic Nessie stare that meant she wasn't backing down. He stared back just as hard, just as intense. Probably more intense since she was driving him crazy. "It was your arousal," he whispered just loud enough for her to hear. "I could smell that you wanted me." And now they both knew it.

CHAPTER TEN

NESSIE HADN'T LOOKED AT CHARLIE FOR THE LAST HALF hour. Dusk had fallen fifteen minutes ago, but she refused to turn and climb out from under the safety of the comforter. What was wrong with her? She hated vampires. Every last bloodsucking one of them. So why in the gods' names had she reacted to Charlie that way? He'd bitten his lip...with his fang. She should've been disgusted by the act, right? Apparently not. But Logan's fangs? Gag. Master's fangs? Double gag, choke, vomit. Charlie's fangs? Turn on? That made no sense.

"Nessie, you have to come out of there eventually." Groaning, she reluctantly threw the covers off her. She could feel Charlie's gaze drilling into her as she walked straight toward the bathroom. Charlie stepped in front of her. "You can't keep ignoring me. We need to work together if we want to get out of here."

She crossed her arms over her chest. "Why are you helping me, anyway? What do you care?" When they'd escaped two nights earlier, she didn't have time to question his motives. He was offering her a way out, and she was taking it. Simple as that. But now the situation felt more complicated. And now she wanted to know what his plan was...and how she fit into it.

Glancing at the floor, he stepped back and shuffled his feet. The long silence that stretched put her on edge, like he didn't want to answer her.

Screw that. She needed to know. She tapped her foot impatiently. "Well?"

He lifted his head, throwing his hands in the air. "What do you want me to say, Ness? We were friends once. Jacques killed your father half out of spite for your stunt in the courtyard. And because your father threatened to kill him. He does not take kindly to threats in any form. And then you go and attack him. I mean, I get why you did it, but you sealed your own death warrant. No way was Jacques going to let you live after that. If I hadn't gotten you out of there, you would have been dead before breakfast. And I... I couldn't let that happen."

Nessie retreated, falling back onto the bed as waves of guilt swept through her. Charlie's words confirmed her own suspicions. If she would have just given Master those damn tears he'd wanted, he might have left her father out of it. "You should've left me in that dungeon," she murmured, curling into a tight ball. "I deserved it." *It should've been me lying in a pool of blood.*

She felt the mattress sink with Charlie's weight next to her. "I couldn't do that, Ness."

"Why not? Because we were friends once upon a time?" She didn't bother trying to keep the sarcasm out of her voice. "That didn't matter when you left."

"I'd like to think we could be friends again."

"Well, we can't!" she screamed, burying her tears in her rage. Now, all of a sudden, he wanted to protect her? *What about ten years ago, you bastard!*

"Why not?" he yelled back, his brows furrowing as ---

"My, my, quite the lovers' spat I've walked in on. What fun. I do love a good bit of drama."

Before she could bolt up in the bed, Charlie's big body was planted in front of her. She heard him mutter "Kat" as she maneuvered to see around him. Sure enough, there stood the dark-haired beauty dressed in red, her matching lips tilted in a half-grin. But Kat's dark eyes narrowed as they landed on her.

Nessie's eyes darted to the window, the quickest way out of the room. They also happened to be on the second floor.

Kat stepped into the room, her attention back on Charlie for the moment. "When Vik called to ask why my beloved Charles had left me for a human, I have to admit I was a little hurt. And I had to come see for myself."

"Does Jacques know?" Charlie snapped.

Kat's face hardened. The fake smile vanishing from her striking features. "Not yet. He seems to think perhaps you're toying with the girl." She flashed an evil eye towards Nessie. "We both know how Jacques likes his games. And you are his favorite student." Darting forward, she got in Charlie's face. "But from what I just witnessed..." She wagged her finger. "Tisk, tisk. Charlie has been a very bad boy."

Kat struck like lightning, her claws catching Nessie across the face and making her stumble back. Charlie caught Kat by the back of the head, dragging her away from Nessie by her hair. He bared his fangs, growling in Kat's face. "You will not touch her again, or it will be the last thing you ever do."

Screaming and clawing at his face, Kat spat obscenities at him. She did not take rejection well. Nessie ran around them and flew out the doorway because if Kat was here, that was her que to leave.

"Goin' somewhere, dearie?"

Nessie screeched to a halt as Viktor stood sneering at her, his beady, red eyes drilling into her. Damn it to hell, these fucking vampires were everywhere! Guess she'd have to resort to her first exit plan. Turning on her heel, she sped back into the bedroom where Charlie was still struggling with Kat. Good gods, why hadn't he killed her yet?

Charlie caught sight of her as she flew by him. "What are you..."

She heard him curse a second before she crashed through the window, the shards of glass nicking and slicing her skin. She braced herself. Falling from a second-story window wasn't going to tickle. But she found herself rolling on impact and was quickly back on her feet, dashing away from the house. A soft thud behind her had her pushing her feet faster.

"Agile lil' thing, aren't ye?" Viktor muttered as he twisted his fist in her hair and yanked her back. That was gonna leave a bald spot. She winced at the pain, but it faded into obscurity as his fangs sank into the meat of her shoulder, tearing through her flesh. She would have taken a thousand lashes in its place. Tears stung her eyes and trickled down her face. She clenched her jaw in agony.

Her arms came up, thumbs finding his eyes and pressing inward with every ounce of strength she could muster. A gurgled roar escaped his mouth as he released her, his grasp loosening enough for her to turn her head. Blood dripped from his eyes as he clenched them shut, releasing her to cover his face. Behind him, she spotted James running from the house towards them.

She bolted. And didn't look back.

This is such fucking insanity, Charlie thought as he grappled with Kat. His crazy ex-girlfriend was clawing his face up while his mate (who didn't even fucking know it yet) was being chased down by a thousand-year-old monster.

"Kat, stop! You're being ridiculous. It's been over ten years. Why do you care who I'm with now?"

"Why do I care? Are you shitting me!" she screamed, flailing in his arms.

"Would you stop clawing at me?!" He grabbed both her arms, pinning them to her sides and glowering at her. "I don't want to hurt you, Kat."

She slouched in his arms, her mouth turning into a giant pout. "Oh, now you don't want to hurt me!"

He let out a sigh of exasperation, rolling his eyes. "I meant physically."

"This is all her fault, isn't it? I'm going to kill her for this!"

Once again, he bared his fangs. "Do not threaten her," he snarled.

Furious determination flared in her eyes as she stared at him. "I will drain that human bitch dry."

Steeling himself against the flood of violent impulses coursing through him, commanding him to slaughter the threat like a rabid dog, he yanked the silver dagger out of his boot. The one he'd bought centuries ago with every last penny his parents had left him. Flipping her onto the ground, he slammed the blade into her chest, missing her heart by mere inches and drawing a hiss from her.

He leaned down, catching sight of the silver webbing rippling out from where the blade was planted. "This is your final warning, Kat. If I catch sight of you near Nessie again, I won't miss your heart next time."

Kat glared up at him, tears sliding down her cheek. The silver would be causing agonizing pain that radiated from the point of impact. And the longer he kept the blade lodged in her flesh, the more widespread the pain. Soon, it would completely immobilize her.

"Why?" she stuttered. "I thought you loved me?"

His gaze softened and he glanced away to compose himself. He couldn't afford to cave to his emotions right now. He took a breath. "Don't play dumb with me, Kat. We both know our kind isn't capable of love without a mate." He looked back at her and felt a twinge of guilt as the webs of silver crept up her face. "Our relationship was never about love."

Her eyes blazed beneath more tears, but this time she couldn't claw at him. Only shed more tears. "Then, you might as well have slammed that dagger home."

"You loved how I fucked you. You never loved me."

"Don't tell me how I felt." Her voice gave way to the pain. She turned her face away, wincing as the webs of silver nearly reached her eyes.

His gut churned as more guilt swamped him. He yanked the dagger out of her chest, and she whimpered with the movement. "Fine. Goodbye, Katherine."

"Fuck you."

Well, that was the problem, now wasn't it. If he'd just kept his dick to himself a decade ago...

He found Viktor outside shrieking with blood streaming down his face. "What the hell happened here?"

James snickered. "Your woman nearly clawed his eyes out. He'll be lucky if he regains vision by the end of the night."

"The sack o' blood nearly blinded me. Why aren't ye draggin' her back here by her entrails?!"

"Well, you deserved it," James spat at him. "You attacked her."

Charlie zoned in on Viktor's face, catching sight of the blood dripping from his mouth. Nessie's blood.

"I can't believe my daughter married such a simpering foo-"

Charlie slammed the bloody dagger still clutched in his fist into Viktor's chest. And he didn't miss the heart this time. Kat was a few decades younger than himself. He could handle her if she didn't heed the only warning she would get. But Viktor. Viktor had centuries on him. He wouldn't get a second chance to eliminate the ancient bastard if they crossed paths again.

And with Nessie's blood in Viktor's system, he could track Nessie down. That couldn't happen.

Someone screamed and Charlie caught sight of Dina running from the house towards them.

"Father? No!" His old friend sobbed as she stood over her father. The silvery webs crept over his body, deteriorating it as they spread.

Dina's watery, blue eyes gazed up at him as she knelt next to Viktor. "You killed my father. In my own house!"

Charlie bowed his head before looking at her again. "He drank from Nessie. I couldn't risk it. I'm sorry."

James crouched down next to his wife, putting his arms around her as he gave Charlie a hard look. But he nodded in understanding as he cradled his sobbing wife in his arms.

"Just go."

Nodding, Charlie took off in search of Nessie, hoping he found her before another monster did.

CHAPTER ELEVEN

A S THE EASTERN SKY SHIFTED FROM BLACK TO INDIGO, THE
stars twinkled out of sight. Dawn was near. And she
was safe...for now. Nessie collapsed in a heap to catch
her breath, wincing as her shoulder protested. The sleeve of her
dark sweater was already soaked with blood.

Glancing around her, she saw nothing but trees, trees, and
more trees. No path. No compass. All she could do was use the
sun to guide her. But where? Her only family was still trapped
with a monster. And her only friend, if she wanted to give Charlie
his way and call him that, had either gone down fighting for her
survival or was about to burn up if he'd been foolish enough to
come after her. She had no one left. Everyone she'd ever even

thought of caring about was gone. And glancing up as the last star vanished in the purple sky, she realized how lost she was without Charlie. She didn't even know which direction to run in, and when the sun crept back out of sight in a few hours, someone would catch up with her. Master, Viktor, or Kat. It didn't matter. She'd pissed off every one of them in one way or another. She'd probably be dead before her next sunrise.

And so, at long last, she curled into a ball on the damp ground and wept. For her father. For herself. For her life unlived.

"No time to cry, Ness. I need to find some shelter. The sun will be up soon."

Her head popped up and she stared at the blurry figure until her vision cleared, and she could see his face. His sweet, handsome face.

"You're alive," she whispered, her voice threatening to crack under the weight of her relief. She threw her arms around his neck, sighing as she felt him solid and real beneath her hands. *You're not going crazy. He's really here.*

"For the time being." His arms slid around her waist, making her gasp. She jumped back, putting a solid foot or two between them.

Blushing, she tucked a strand of hair behind her ear, feeling her cheeks heat.

They stood there in silence, but she kept catching a glance of Charlie's barely-contained smile. Finally, he said, "I really do need to find shelter."

She nodded. "Lead the way."

Charlie found a cave not far away and snuck inside first. A roar echoed from inside, making her jump and dash behind a tree. A few moments later, a large cat came scurrying out of the cave and into the woods behind her. Charlie appeared in the entrance, beckoning her to him. Once inside, she followed him deeper into the cave where there was almost no light. But she could still make out the shadows that outlined the tunnel. He slipped his hand inside hers, tugging her forward.

"Why do you insist on leading me like a toddler?" she huffed but didn't remove her hand. It was a small comfort having the physical connection to prove he was really here. Not a pile of ash. Not a figment of a desperate mind. "I know you missed the last decade, but I'm all grown up now."

He turned his head back to look at her. The shadows of his face moved as he gave her a sly smile that he probably thought she couldn't see. "Trust me. I've noticed."

Heat rose in her cheeks as Charlie began trekking forward again.

They walked for what seemed like forever. She forgot herself, glancing around the dark tunnel. There were veins of sparkling stones running along the cave walls. Which made her crash into Charlie's backside when he suddenly stopped, and she stumbled backwards. Clumsy idiot. Charlie's hand tightened around hers and, with a small jerk, she found herself in his arms as he straightened her. "Watch yourself."

She hissed as his hand glided over her injured shoulder, hidden beneath her black, blood-soaked sweater. "Gods, Nessie! I could smell you were bleeding, but not like this. Why didn't you tell me he mauled you?!"

She wrenched herself from his arms, but he held tight to her hand. "We had more pressing matters."

"Well, I'm taking care of that before we rest for the day." She opened her mouth. "Don't argue!" he snapped before leading further into the cave. Taking care of it? What the hell did that mean?

Charlie's hands pulled on the collar of her sweater, his breath on her face. She shivered as he swept the material away, revealing her damaged skin. She knew what he was about to do. And...she didn't stop it. The distinct memory of him healing her wrist crossed her mind. She realized with a twinge of horror that she didn't *want* to stop it this time.

His tongue slid over her shoulder and she sucked in a breath, waiting for the feel of sharp fangs sinking into her. But it didn't come. Only the blissful warmth of his mouth against her cool skin. She found herself leaning into him, craving more. He shuddered and then his mouth left her skin, and she almost whimpered at the loss.

"I have to stop. I don't want to do more damage than good," he whispered as he leaned away from her. His hand, which she hadn't even realized rested on her leg, moved away.

He'd wanted to bite her. And, yet he'd forced himself away. She worried her bottom lip between her teeth, her mind and body fighting for control. She wanted nothing to do with his mouth. Nothing, dammit!

Trying to distract herself, she reached up and touched her shoulder, finding it almost completely healed. His tongue had swept almost all the blood away, and his mouth had healed most of the wound.

"Thanks," she said. Good gods, was that breathless voice hers?!

"You're welcome." His voice was low and sexy. The voice that went with his black eyes. The knowledge sent her body into another tidal wave of heat, and she gritted her teeth as she turned away.

"Well, I'll see you in a few hours, then." She lay herself on the cold, hard ground, wishing for the soft bed she had enjoyed only the day before.

"Sleep well," Charlie whispered before the cave fell into silence.

Charlie dreamt of the woman beside him. It was the second time he'd sensed her arousal in as many days. Maybe she didn't hate him after all.

They settled into another underground cavern the following morning. Charlie watched as Nessie collapsed beside him. He'd carried her despite her objections.

"We already lost a day back at Dina's because of Viktor. We can't afford to go at your pace," he'd said as he'd hauled her ass off the ground and took off.

She curled into a ball and fell asleep. When he caught sight of her shivering, a lump lodged in his throat. He scooted in as close to her as he could without risking waking her, hoping his waning body heat would suffice.

He tried to sleep, but his own body was restless. And with his mate only inches away, he practically hummed with anticipation. His morning wood was turning into all-day wood. Ridiculous. He was losing control of his own body. Not good.

When he heard the soft pitter-patter of footsteps, he scrambled to his feet, planting himself in front of Nessie. She groaned, nudging him with her elbow.

"Charlie, what the—"

He shushed her, and, by some miracle, she fell silent. For about five seconds.

"What's wrong?" she whispered.

"There's someone in the upper part of the cave."

Suddenly, the soft footsteps above were drowned out by the sound of Nessie's frantic heartbeat. "They've found us, haven't they?" she asked, a tremor in her voice.

"I doubt it. It's still a few hours until sunset. They'd all be dust if they were up there right now."

No, whomever paced in the cavern above was no vampire. And that didn't make him any less wary. Because he wasn't the only monster with fangs in these woods.

"It seems to be staying up there for now. Try to get some more rest."

Nessie snorted and crossed her arms over her chest. Leaning back against the cave wall, she stared up at the ceiling.

He shook his head, taking a seat next to her. They sat, quietly waiting for the sun to set.

"Why did you come after me?" she asked, breaking the hours of silence.

He glanced over at her, finding her staring at him.

"After I ran from Dina's. Why did you come after me?"

"I get the feeling you didn't want me to."

"I didn't say that, and that's not an answer."

When he saw the determined look on his face, he sighed. "Risking the sun was worth finding you before someone else did."

"It wouldn't have been if you'd burned up."

"I guess fate was on our side, then."

Charlie could sense the exact moment the sun had disappeared behind the mountains. Time to find out who was blocking their only way out.

Thankfully, he'd taken in a few teaspoons of Nessie's blood when he'd healed her shoulder. Those few precious ounces had given his strength back even as it robbed him of some much-needed control.

"Stay here. I'll come back when I know what we're dealing with," he whispered. He dashed off before she could argue.

He crept up, inching his way towards the opening of the cave. Peeking his head around the corner, he tried to locate the threat, but the cave looked empty. Wary of the sudden disappearance, he tip-toed towards the entrance.

Just as he was about to peer out into the dark woods, a large, white wolf jumped in front of him, teeth bared, hackles raised in full alarm. He flashed his lengthening fangs at the animal, growling his own warning. Most animals would easily recognize his kind as the superior predator and flee. This one growled back and snapped its teeth at him instead. Not a good sign.

As the two of them circled each other, trying to find an opening for an attack, Charlie heard more footsteps behind him. With the wolf in front of him, he didn't bother glancing back. An all-too familiar and alluring scent wafted through the air thick with tension.

"I told you to stay down there," he snapped. The wolf's icy gaze flickered behind him for a moment.

He caught Nessie shrug out of the corner of his eye. "I decided not to listen."

The wolf barked and he saw a smile curve its snout. Then, his initial suspicion was confirmed. The wolf was no more. In its place stood a tall, ivory-skinned woman with hair as pale as the wolf's fur and eyes the same icy blue. She wore a sly smile and nothing else. No surprise there. Lycans couldn't transform clothes.

"Is the girl with you?" the woman asked, her voice soft and wispy.

Charlie nodded stiffly.

She nodded in return. "A neighboring pack has caught your scent. They're tailing you. No pun intended."

Charlie's arms fell to his sides. "Why are you warning us?"

The woman's eyes saddened as her eyes locked onto Nessie, pity pooling in their depths. "I know how this pack operates. When she's caught, they will enslave her." Her eyes shifted back to his face. "They will kill you on sight, bloodsucker. She slows you down. You will never outrun them with her. Leave her."

"No." There was no hesitation in his response. No way in hell would have been a more accurate response, but he wanted to keep this conversation as short as possible.

A smile curved her mouth. "You must care for the girl, then."

Charlie paused, his eyes darting to Nessie for just a

moment. More than she realized. When his gaze flickered back to the woman, he nodded.

"If the pack kills you, she won't stand a chance. But if you leave her behind, the pack knows they won't be able to catch up with you. They'll abandon their hunt for you once they find her. It's not you they want. It's her. You're just an obstacle."

Charlie's jaw clenched as he mulled her words over.

She tilted her head, her eyes widening frightfully large. "The pack is coming. Choose quickly. Your time is running out." With that, she shifted back into the white wolf and took off into the night.

Charlie glanced back at Nessie, her eyes drilling into his. He grabbed her hand and squeezed, praying she'd understand.

"I need to leave."

She pulled her hand from his grasp. "What?"

He pressed his lips together and he saw her eyes start to glisten. "We can't risk both of us being caught."

Her eyes narrowed on him. "You mean *you* can't risk getting caught."

"I can't save you if I'm dead," he pressed. "I have to go."

She closed her eyes and a tear slid down her cheek. "I can't become a slave again. I just...I can't." She opened her eyes, shining as the moonlight reflected off her unshed tears. "Please..."

Don't leave me. Her unspoken words rang in his mind. The streaks running down her cheeks clawed at his resolve. But the she-wolf was right. If he stayed with her, they'd both be caught.

And if he left now, it might be the last time he ever saw her. If his split-second plan didn't work. *No*, he thought. *It must work. But just in case...*

He placed a hand on the back of her neck, pulling her into him. His mouth landed on hers and he swallowed her gasp of shock. But she didn't pull away. She sank into him, pressing her body against him. His other hand slid up her back so he could hold her close, feeling her heart beating against his chest. He dove into her mouth with the intensity befitting a first and (potentially) final kiss. If this was his only chance, he was giving her everything he had.

And she absorbed every ounce of it, giving it back as if her life depended on it. Her tongue slid over one of his fangs, and he moaned into her mouth, clutching her tighter to him.

But as much as he wanted this to last. It couldn't. In the far distance, his keen hearing picked up a faint howling. Mentally cursing, he forced himself to pull his mouth from the blissful heat of hers. In the cold night air, his lips still burned with the fire of that one kiss. A kiss he'd never forget no matter how long he lived.

He rested his forehead on hers, his eyes still closed as he took a breath. "I will always come back for you, Nessie," he whispered...and then he was gone.

CHAPTER TWELVE

NESSIE OPENED HER EYES, FINDING HIM VANISHING IN A blur. She tried to catch the breath that kiss had taken, her fingers skimming across her tingling lips. Her first kiss. That certainly wasn't the way she imagined her first kiss with Charlie going. Not that she imagined kissing Charlie...much.

A howl sounded, faint and far away, jolting her from her thoughts. She shook herself and ran in the direction Charlie had vanished. Stupid woman. Gushing over a goodbye kiss. From the same guy that had vanished in a blur just like this.

Ten years earlier...

Nessie skipped out of her family's room and headed for the kitchen. It was dark. Which meant her favorite person (well, one of them) was finally awake.

"Mommy, have you seen Charlie?"

Her mother turned from the stove and smiled down at her. "No, honey. He's probably still in Miss Kat's room."

Nessie wrinkled her nose. She did not like Miss Kat. That vampire lady was always mean to her mommy. Plus, she didn't like how she kept touching Charlie. Gag.

She went and hopped on her father's lap. He hugged her. "Daddy, can you get Charlie out of Miss Kat's room?"

Her father glanced up at her mother. "I'm afraid not, sweetie."

Nessie sighed and slumped against her father's chest.

"Eva."

Nessie felt her father straighten up, standing from the chair and pulling Nessie behind him in one movement. Peeking around her father's leg, she watched wide-eyed as Master swept into the room, his blond hair disheveled and his pale eyes sweeping over her mother. Nessie gulped and looked at her mother.

Her mother turned away from the stove and gazed up into Master's face. "Yes, Jack?"

Nessie tilted her head. She always wondered why her mother was the only one that ever dared to call Master by name.

Master remained silent, merely holding out his hand. Her mother glanced at her father and down to her for a moment before slipping her hand into Master's. When Master started pulling her mother out of the room, Nessie tried to step around her father.

"Mommy?"

Her father held her in place as she craned around him to stare at her mother, who turned her head and gave her a smile. "I'll be back in a little while, honey. Be good for your father."

As her mother and Master disappeared from the room, she looked up at her father's sunken face. She glared at the doorway.

Why did her mother keep leaving with Master when it made her father so sad?

"I don't like when Mommy leaves with Master," she said, clutching her father's leg as she tried not to cry.

Her father knelt and wiped his cheek. "I know, sweetie. But sometimes people have to do things they don't like to protect the ones they love."

Nessie gave her father a confused look.

He stroked her cheek. "You'll understand when you're older."

Nessie sniffled and pulled from his embrace. "I'm going to find Charlie." She turned on her heel and ran from the room in search of her best friend. He'd tell her why Master kept stealing her Mommy away. He knew Master better than anyone.

She even dared to knock on Miss Kat's door.

The door flew open, and Miss Kat stood there in a red dress that seemed completely pointless since Nessie could see right through it anyway. Miss Kat's smile vanished as her eyes fell to Nessie. She rolled her eyes. "What do you want, kid?"

"Is Charlie here?"

A fleeting look of sadness crossed Miss Kat's face before it vanished. "No. Master sent him away a few minutes ago."

Nessie jaw fell. Charlie's leaving?

"When will he be back?" she asked.

Miss Kat narrowed her eyes. "I don't even have that information. What makes you think you're entitled to it?"

Nessie stumbled back and shook her head. "Nevermind. Sorry." She dashed away, heading for the front door. He wouldn't leave her. Not without saying goodbye at least. Maybe she missed him. Maybe he'd come to her room after she'd left. While she was in the kitchen with her parents. But why wouldn't he come find her?

She skidded down the stairs, nearly tripping over the last one as she spotted him. He grabbed a large bag from Bobby and nodded. Then he vanished.

"No! Charlie!" She flew through the foyer and ran outside into the darkness. "Charlie! Come back!" But he was just a streak that disappeared into the distance.

I will always come back for you, Nessie. Charlie's last words rang in her ears as her feet ate up as much distance as her human legs could manage.

She couldn't wait another ten years for him to make good on his promise. She fought back tears as she heard the howls somewhere in the distance behind her. The trees around her grew blurry and her foot caught on a root she couldn't see through her wretched tears. She tumbled, landing in the dirt.

Why was she even running? The wolves were faster than her, Charlie was faster than her. What was the point of running at all? They would catch her, and Charlie was long gone. She cursed him for leaving her behind...again. And there was no way she was screaming for him to come back this time, not with supernatural senses honing in on her.

Another howl rang out, this one closer than before, and that had her back on her feet.

She could hear a crowd of paws pounding against the ground behind her, growing louder every minute. It wouldn't be long now. There was no outrunning them. She glanced up, the intertwining branches above her offering little hope, but she'd take any right now.

Leaping, she wrapped her fingers around a thick branch and pulled herself up. She found her footing and moved to the next branch, climbing quickly. Glancing below, she made out a small group of wolves heading her way. When they reached the base of her tree, clawing at the trunk and snapping their jaws up at her, she turned away and continued climbing. One barked loudly.

Branches trembled beneath her, and she glanced down in time to see a man reach out and grab her ankle, yanking her off her own branch. She screamed, falling into the man's grasp. His face was emotionless as he looked down at her, his eyes bored, almost empty. Flailing in a desperate attempt to save herself, she landed a solid hit to his face as her palm shoved into his nose. He roared as he released her, clutching his nose. She grunted as her body broke through a branch, probably cracking a rib on her descent to the ground.

Arms as round as some of the branches she'd just climbed caught her easily. "This one's a fighter," the man said in a low, booming voice. He set her on her feet, and she winced as sharp agony tore through her side. She clutched it with one arm, his large hand still wrapped around the other. She glared up at him, way up. Her jaw fell slack as she stared.

He was the largest man she'd ever seen, towering over her by at least two feet, and he had to weigh more than three hundred pounds. The man was just...giant. He smiled down at her, the corners of his black eyes crinkling, but his gaze held no warmth, just cold humor at her helplessness.

Black waves fell over his forehead as he gazed down at her. "Leroy," he called. "Take her back to the village. The rest of us need to hunt. We'll be back in the morning."

Another man stepped forward, taking her arms as she was shoved toward him. He turned her and she caught sight of the large man shrinking...until an enormous black wolf stood in his place.

The pack didn't hesitate as they followed their leader away deeper into the woods as Leroy pulled her along in the other direction. She followed in silence, having no interest in speaking to her captor.

They reached the village in less than an hour. It was small and primitive. Nothing like the luxuriousness of the mansion she grew up in. Small, wooden houses were scattered within a hundred feet of one another. Dirt paths ran between them. A few small buildings stood on the edge of the village, and a large ring of rocks were placed in the center with a pile of logs and branches inside. She could see several women flitting in and out of the houses, carrying crude dinnerware and clothing.

Leroy led her through the village, throwing her inside a small shed.

"In here," he snapped before shutting the door. The lock clicked, confirming her imprisonment. She darted over to the small window, trying to push it up and open. But the damn thing wouldn't budge. It was locked tight. Stupid thing was too small to climb through anyway, so she didn't know why she'd bothered. And gave herself a few splinters in the process. She cursed loudly.

Someone gasped behind her, making her spin on her heel. She squinted in the dimly lit room, spotting another woman, not much older than herself by the looks of her, crouched in the far corner of the room. A scrap of a blanket lay in front of her.

Nessie kept her distance, watching the woman with a wary eye. But she simply stayed in her corner, shaking like a leaf with her hands over her ears. Her chest twisted with pity as she realized the poor thing was probably another slave. And one who had been through way too much. Her long, red hair was in a wild tangle around her slender face, which was smudged with dirt and other bright colors. That was when Nessie noticed the large mural on the wall behind the woman.

"Did you paint that?" Nessie asked as she admired the mural of a field of bright wildflowers. When the woman didn't answer, Nessie took a step towards the woman. Instantly, the woman's body shook harder, and she clenched her bright, green eyes shut. *Okay. Keep my distance, then.* Nessie backed up, sliding down the opposite wall and taking a seat.

"It's a beautiful painting," Nessie continued in a soft voice.

She spent the next hour trying to coax the woman into a conversation. But she wouldn't cooperate, her lips clamped shut tight as a fist. Nessie huffed in defeat and curled into a ball on the floor; praying to anyone who would listen that she wouldn't end up like the poor woman across the room.

"C'mon, female. Up!"

Her eyes snapped open, and she blinked away the blurriness as a hand hoisted her up from the floor. Leroy was back and dragging her out of the room. She glanced back in time to catch a tear falling from the woman's eyes as she watched Nessie be dragged from the room.

He tightened his grip. "C'mon, move it!" She sped up trying to keep up with him. Bumps broke out over her exposed skin in the cold night air. A large fire blazed in the stone circle with a crowd standing on one side. Mostly males stood huddled together, a few women and children dotted in between. Leroy pulled her around it and a large boulder came into view. The black wolf, now a giant man once again, stood atop it.

"Jaxon," Leroy called. He pulled Nessie in front of him, nodding in her direction.

The giant turned toward them, motioning them forward before he turned to whisper to the man beside him. Leroy led her up the makeshift steps onto the boulder, halting her just in front of Jaxon. She shook Leroy's arm off, narrowing her gaze on Jaxon as he stared down at her.

Jaxon's eyebrow lifted, the corners of his lips curving into a smirk. "This one has a stubborn streak." He watched her a few moments longer, then, crossed his arms over his chest, his smile vanishing. "Strip."

Her breath hitched and she blinked up at him. She must have heard him wrong, she told herself. He couldn't have said...

"You heard me, female. Strip, now." He lowered his face down to within inches of hers, a hint of smile creeping back onto his face. "Or I'll be more than happy to help you."

She took several steps back, her body crashing into the other man behind her. Her eyes darted around her, searching for a way out. She tried to run, but the man behind her caught her arm and held her tight. She would not strip! No way in hell would she do it willingly.

Her elbow slammed behind her, making contact with the man's stomach. Her hand followed suit, fist connecting with groin. She heard an ooof and a groan before the hand that gripped her arm released her. She turned on her heel, her knee coming up and smashing into his face. He reeled back. She made to run off the side of the boulder toward the woods, but those tree-trunk size arms enveloped her, squeezing until she could just barely breathe. As her lungs started seizing painfully through her hyperventilating, she tried to kick the giant bastard that held her.

"You were right about that stubborn streak," Leroy said to Jaxon as he watched her struggle. She caught sight of the other man clutching his nose, which was gushing blood through his fingers. His eyes held murder as he glared at her. She smirked as her eyes met his, relishing the justified bloodshed.

Jaxon growled low. "She is strong for one so small." Her vision started to go fuzzy, and as much as she wanted to continue her struggle, her body weakened with lack of air and she slumped in his arms. He handed her off to Leroy. "Hold her still."

Turning toward the crowd, he held his arms up and the chatter died. "Human female. Young, ripe, and a little feisty if that's your thing." She caught him winking at the crowd, and a few masculine chuckles rang out in return. "Any takers?" A dozen sets of eyes landed on her, scrutinizing her like a piece of livestock.

Facing her again, he shoved a finger at her. "Do not struggle again. Or you will regret it. I promise." His hands grasped the hem of her shirt, pulling it over her head.

She could hear men shouting in the crowd, calling out bids, but she blocked them out. Their voices muted as Jaxon's hands grasped the sides of her jeans. Her underwear slid down as he peeled them off her. She swung her foot up, slamming it against his chin. Her foot exploded in agony as his head jerked up.

He lowered his face, his eyes glowering with the promise of pain.

She forced a smile at him. "Sorry, muscle spasm," she said in the sweetest voice she could muster.

He stared at her a moment before his booming laugh rang out.

"Definitely a feisty one," Leroy said.

Jaxon's fingers reached behind her and found the clasps to her bra. Unsnapping them with his big, clumsy fingers took longer than he was willing to wait, and he ended up tearing the material off her instead. He gazed down at her, stepping back as his eyes roved over her naked body. Shaking inside, her eyes burned with unshed tears. Instead, she lifted her chin and locked gazes with him. His lips curved into a grin. "Feisty, indeed," he rumbled, running his fingers over his five o-clock shadow.

He turned to face the crowd again, holding a hand up. The men shouting bids fell silent. Straightening himself to his full height, he puffed out his barrel-sized chest. "She is mine."

A rush of breath escaped her, her eyes scanning the crowd. But no one dared challenge his claim on her.

He turned back, his black eyes drilling into her. "And I will enjoy my prize now."

Her eyes widened and she clenched her jaw as he took a single step toward her. Her whole body tensed at his approach.

"Don't touch me." Her foot came up, but he anticipated it this time, his long fingers wrapping around her ankle. He jerked and Leroy released her. She lost her balance and fell onto the boulder. Jaxon was on her in a moment, scooping her up and throwing her over his massive shoulders. The struggles she made did little to faze him and off the ground she found little leverage to use against him.

His fingers inched up her calf as he carried her away from the crowd and into the line of trees behind it. Her struggles intensified. "Get your hands off me!" she screamed as she slammed a fist onto his back.

He grunted but chuckled a moment later. "I do love a challenge." He tightened his grip on her, barely giving her room to wriggle, let alone fight back. After several minutes of him walking and her struggling with little effect, he finally set her on her feet, her back pressed against the trunk of a tree. But a moment later, her feet were off the ground again as he lifted her, forcing his thigh between her legs.

He snatched her wrists, holding them above her head as his face lowered toward her own. She turned away, his breath tickling her neck. She felt him readjusting, one large hand now holding both of her small wrists above her as his other hand came down and forced her face to turn back toward his own. His mouth pressed against hers, trying to force her lips open. She complied, her teeth chomping down as she tasted blood. And, oh, it tasted good. Vengeance, even this small act, was truly sweet.

He yelped at the pain, pulling his face back. His eyes glowed, a frightening gold as his bleeding lips curved into a grin. He leaned back in and she slammed her head against his, groaning in agony. Dots blanketed her vision. And she hoped she didn't just give herself a concussion. Because this pig had a skull like a boulder.

And hands like giant sandpaper that grated against her skin.

Oh, gods. Is this really happening? Her first intimate experience would be like *this*? What the fuck did the universe have against her?!

The sound of a zipper echoed through her ears like a cannon.

"Please," she begged, opening her eyes still blurry from the impact. "I'm still a---"

But before she could finish the sentence a branch cracked above their heads. They both snapped their heads to look up. She could make out a dark-haired male leaping from the branches above them. He landed on Jaxon's back, his fangs sinking deep into the larger man's jugular. His red eyes drew her gaze as her head lulled from the pain. Charlie?

Jaxon released her and she fell to the ground as he stumbled backward with Charlie still on his back. He roared and reached up to tear the vampire off him, but Charlie was too fast, ripping out a chunk of flesh before sinking his fangs into the other side of his neck and tearing through another couple of layers. When Charlie released him again, his fist smashed into Jaxon's skull. Jaxon fell onto the ground, his hands clamping over the wounds at his neck. Her eyes struggled to focus on Charlie standing over the fallen giant.

Blood coated the lower half of his face as it slid down his chin and neck. His eyes glowed a bright red, even more terrifying than Jaxon's had looked a moment ago. That frightening gaze snapped back to her, making her breath hitch. It was the first time she'd seen Charlie look...like a monster.

He rushed over to her and she tried to scurry back, gasping as her head protested. Snatching her up from the cold ground, she wanted to gag at the traces of blood smearing onto her body as he raced away with her. But her body didn't want to cooperate, her head falling back as the world went black.

CHAPTER
THIRTEEN

THAT FUCKING ANIMAL. HE'D TOUCHED HER. *HIS* HER. THE beast had tried to claim what was his. By force. It had brought out the monster within his own soul. The one that thirsted for blood and violence. His vision blanketed in raw, red rage before he struck the mongrel as he violated Nessie. The fact that he was the largest lycan Charlie had ever seen didn't matter a bit. He had the element of surprise and struck before the lycan had a chance to shift. Watching the beast crumple beneath him brought a primal satisfaction, but one he couldn't revel in as his eyes found Nessie sprawled on the ground, struggling to remain conscious.

He tried not to look at her body, stripped and bared for all to see. But as he picked her up, he couldn't stop his eyes from taking in every sweet curve. Her ribs jutted out, making him curse himself to hell and back. Her need for food had slipped his mind. Having not eaten a morsel in a few centuries, it was no wonder. But that was no excuse. He had to do better. He would do better. For her.

You don't have time to ogle her right now, he told himself over and over. *Ogle her later, move now!* His gaze tracked the blood that smeared across her chest as he tucked her against him and hauled ass out of there. Before the giant's friends came looking.

He took shelter in yet another damp, dreary cave. These mountains were littered with them. One of the reasons he'd chosen this particular path.

Laying her down for a moment, he stripped his shirt off and wiped the blood off his face. As he cleaned Nessie's body of any trace of blood, he noticed the nasty lump forming on her forehead and wished he had ripped that giant barbarian's throat out. When they were both as clean as he could manage, he sat against the wall and pulled her unconscious body against his own, draping the shirt over both of them. The mongrel's blood still burned through his system, providing them both with some much-needed body heat. Eventually, after watching her for a while, he drifted off himself, his dreams once again occupied by the woman in his arms.

Nessie sighed as she nestled closer to the source of heat that blanketed her. She hadn't been this warm and cozy since snuggling between her parents as a child. She peeled her eyes open but was greeted only by darkness. Shifting, she felt an arm draped over her, tightening and pulling her closer as she tried to nudge it off her. Images of Jaxon's arms holding her still for his assault flashed through her mind and she scrambled to her feet. The cold air hit her like a knife, taking her breath away and clearing her foggy mind. Jaxon had been sprawled on the ground just before she'd blacked out.

"Nessie?"

A rush of relief swept through her as the familiar voice called out. She reached out in the darkness, her eyes adjusting slowly. "Charlie?"

"Nessie, you're freezing —"

"Y-you came back for me," she whispered, stunned by how happy she sounded. His face slowly came into focus...along with the rest of him. Why didn't he have a shirt on?

"I told you I would. Didn't you believe me?"

His arms and chest flexed as he reached up and stroked her cheek. *Don't stare. Do not stare.* She knew the man was attractive, but...whoa. Hello, gorgeous. Thank the gods she hadn't seen him shirtless back when she'd actually crushed on him. She'd have been a goner for sure.

She cleared the lump from her throat and tried to sound indifferent. "I probably would've left you there." Probably.

"Guess that just means I'm a better friend than you are, then."

"Yeah, guess so."

"Are you actually admitting that we're friends now?" he asked, though there was a hint of surprise in his voice.

She shrugged. "Maybe."

"Ahhh, sweet progress."

She nudged him in the shoulder. "I said maybe, not yes."

"Hey, that's better than a no, right?"

She rolled her eyes at him. Smart ass.

"Look, as much as I am thoroughly enjoying the view, you really should put my shirt on before you freeze to death."

Her hands slapped over her chest, skimming over her bare skin. Holy gods, she was still naked!

"Allow me," Charlie whispered in her ear from behind, making her jump. How had he gotten behind her so fast? Oh, right. Vampire.

"Dammit, would you stop doing that!"

He chuckled. "Doing what? Dressing you? I wouldn't mind if you stayed naked, but in this weather, I wouldn't advise it."

She whipped around to face him, her nipples brushing against his chest. They both sucked in a sharp breath and she took a hurried step back. Pleasure bolted through her, streaking straight to her core and taking the chill with it. Her body flushed with heat despite the piercing cold around her.

Snatching the shirt from him, she threw it over her shoulders fumbling with the buttons. Her frozen fingers didn't seem to want to cooperate.

"Here, let me help." His warm fingers slid over hers before pushing her hands out of the way. She had the urge to slap his hands away, but the heat was too enticing to resist. And she really did want the shirt buttoned as soon as possible. "You know," he whispered, breaking the silence, his voice cascading over her. The voice that meant his eyes were black. "This shirt isn't going to keep your bottom half warm. Maybe I should give you the rest of my clothes, too."

Breathe in. Breathe out. Nice and steady. Do not hyperventilate. Heat radiated from him as he lingered with each button. She wanted to bask in that warmth, melt into it, absorb as much as she could get her hands on. And nothing was stopping her, nothing but herself.

She raised her hand, skimming her palm across his knuckles. His fingers paused on the last button as she brushed up his arm, feeling his muscles flex beneath her fingers.

"Nessie..." he whispered in the dark.

"Shhh." His feverish skin felt like he'd been dipped in sunshine, and as all that lean muscle slid beneath her touch, the last chill in her body vanished.

She shouldn't. Really. But she stepped forward, closing the small gap that had remained between them. Pressing her body against his. Wrapping herself around him as she laid her head on his shoulder, the tip of her nose grazing along the column of his neck.

"Thank you," she murmured against his skin. *For coming back this time.*

Speechless, and more than a little aroused, Charlie slowly wrapped his arms around Nessie. The incident with the lycan had put his protective instincts into high gear, which only made him want to claim her more. The mark of a vampire's mate offered some protection in itself. Only those with a death wish would dare harm a marked mate. Tales of entire villages slaughtered over the murder of a mate made most reluctant to even make eye contact. He smiled, running his hand through her hair and toying with her ear.

"That's what friends are for," he whispered. Friends...yeah. Because that's definitely where his head was at right now.

He caught her smile, and wanted to stand there and hold her forever, but they had a lot more distance to put between themselves and their growing list of enemies.

"We should get going now that the sun has set," he bit out, hating to have to ruin the moment. Who knew when or if he'd get to enjoy another like it anytime soon.

Nessie lifted her head, searching for his face. "Of course. You're right," she said, nodding.

He took another moment to enjoy the look on her face as his thumb caressed her cheek. Then, he led her up into the upper cavern of the cave. Moonlight filtered into the cave as he set her down, scanning for danger, and finding his eyes continually distracted back to her.

His keen senses revealed no imminent danger. He turned, allowing his eyes to settle on her. His shirt, which was far too thin for this kind of weather, fell just low enough to hide her delectably-rounded rear from sight. Stupid shirts had to ruin everything.

He watched her as her eyes roamed from his face downward, taking in his naked torso, his cock twitching back to life as he saw the glimmer of attraction sweep across her eyes. "Ready?"

Her gaze snapped back up to his face before she glanced away and nodded.

He lifted her into his arms.

She tried to wriggle from his grasp. "I can still walk, you caveman."

He smiled, tightening his hold on her. "True, but you need heat, or you'll freeze to death. Now, I can think of a multitude of other ways I'd prefer to keep you warm, but that will have to wait until daybreak." Her cheeks flushed at his blatant insinuation, and he tucked her a little closer to him. "Besides, you didn't mind snuggling up against all this hotness two minutes ago."

He set off before she could protest any further, not that that would have changed anything. Without his body heat, she could easily lose a few toes or worse. So, like it or not, he was carrying her. Within a few minutes, Nessie stopped fidgeting and relaxed against him.

Not long before sunrise, Charlie slowed as he saw the faint glow of firelight in the distance. He stopped, sensing something stirring in the trees. Silently setting Nessie on her feet, he stepped in front of her, shielding her from whomever lurked in the shadows.

The swoosh of a hand ripped through the silence and Charlie turned in time to see a fist coming at his face. He ducked, pushing Nessie out of the way, but his jaw got clipped as he maneuvered around.

A vampire. And few of his own kind lived alone. Most sought protection in covens that dwelled in the cities. The forests belonged to the lycans. Only poachers, vampires who made a living catching humans to sell into the slave market, made a habit of venturing into the woods. Usually in groups. His eyes flickered behind the stranger, waiting for another to creep out from the darkness.

Many vampires were too poor to own slaves. The poorest survived on animal blood, while those with better means usually kept bagged blood handy. Only the wealthiest could afford to buy and maintain a blood slave. Which was why poaching had become such a popular profession in recent years.

He crouched, ready to spring at yet another stranger that threatened to steal his mate.

CHAPTER FOURTEEN

NESSIE BACKED AWAY AS CHARLIE STRUCK AT THE NEWCOMER. By the looks of how the two went at it, they were dealing with another vampire. Fan-fucking-tastic.

Nessie turned, ready to flee. The last thing she needed was another monster getting their hands on her. Not like the last few times had worked out so great.

"Watch! There could be more of them," Charlie called, grunting as he took another blow to the face.

There were more?! Oh, joy. She gazed around, not finding any others, but she knew that didn't mean much. As she twirled looking for more threats, she realized...she didn't have a fucking clue which way was north.

When she heard Charlie roar, flying into the trunk of a tree and landing on his ass, she cursed. If he lost this fight...

Her chest squeezed at the thought. She couldn't leave him here to die. Besides, she needed his navigation skills....and protection it would seem.

Turning back towards the two admittedly gorgeous monsters brawling, she sighed. If she lived through this...they were even. No more reason to feel all warm and cozy and grateful for saving her ass. On more than one occasion, but that wasn't the point.

She was doing this for her. For her life. For her father. For her freedom. This had nothing to do with him, or any other vampire. And she sure as hell wasn't going to let them stand in her way now.

Charging with bare feet through the snow (she was going to regret that later), she leapt onto the stranger's back. But he flung her off him like a pesky rodent, turning to stare at her.

"Why haven't you run from your Master?"

The question took her (and Charlie from the look on his face) by such surprise, that they both froze.

"He...he's not my Master," she stuttered.

"Nessie!" Charlie snapped. "Don't say that. He'll think you're fair game!"

"Is she yours then?" the stranger asked.

Charlie's gaze locked onto the stranger's as he lowered the fist he was about to throw into the stranger's face. "Yes," he growled. "She's mine."

The possessive tone he used made her want to swoon...and rip his vocal cords out. She scowled, huffing loudly as she crossed her arms over her chest.

The stranger frowned, disapproval in the hard lines of his face. His eyes narrowed on Charlie. "Where are her clothes? Your shirt isn't sufficient for this kind of weather."

"A...umm...wolf---man took them," Nessie blurted.

Anger filtered into the stranger's expression as he looked at Charlie again. "She is your responsibility, and you allow a lycan to..."

Nessie stepped towards them. "He didn't allow it! He risked his life to save me from that monster!" The stranger's eyes widened in surprise. And why the hell was she defending Charlie anyway? He'd just staked another fucking claim on her!

"If you aren't a poacher, please allow us to pass. I need to get her somewhere safe before sunrise," Charlie said.

The stranger surveyed the two of them for long moments. "Fine. I have some spare clothes the woman can have. She'll be frozen to death before you get to safety if you leave her dressed like that." He turned, motioning for them to follow. And muttering under his breath about incompetent fledglings who didn't know how lucky they were.

Nessie went to follow the stranger, but Charlie scooped her up again.

"If you keep this up, I'm gonna forget how to walk."

Charlie shrugged, "I'm perfectly capable of carrying you for the rest of your life."

She gaped at him, speechless. Because the idea of being confined to his arms forever sounded terrifying, and kinda perfect.

Don't do it. No, she couldn't let herself be drawn in again. She'd done that before, being as young and naïve as she'd been it was no wonder. But she'd gotten over her heartbreak, and now was not the time to tear those walls down.

Charlie set her down in front of a large tent where a thick rug lay in front of the entrance. The stranger emerged from the tent with an armful of clothes.

Nessie smiled at him and held her hand out. "I'm Nessie." The man was saving her from frostbite, so the least she could do was introduce herself. Though, she secretly wondered why a vampire (especially one she didn't know personally) would care if she got frostbite. Her thoughts turned to Dina, the friendliest vampire she'd ever met, and the amazing shower and clothes she'd given Nessie without hesitation. Maybe some vampires weren't *all* bad.

The stranger stared at her hand, hesitating for a moment before shifting the clothes and placing his dark hand in hers. "Raul." He offered a thick, wool sweater, leather leggings, and some oversized boots for her. "You can change in the tent," he said.

Nessie took the clothes with a quick thanks and eyed the tent.

"Unless you'd rather change out here in the open that is," he continued, making Charlie scowl and clench his fist. Apparently, he didn't like the idea of the stranger seeing her naked. *Good, that makes two of us.* Climbing inside the tent, she was amazed by how warm it was inside. Must be the super shiny fabric holding all the heat in.

"She looks like you haven't fed her in a week. What's wrong with you?" Raul snapped loud enough for even her ears to hear. She clenched her teeth. It wasn't Charlie's job to feed her. She wasn't his fucking pet. But that got her thinking...when was the last time she'd eaten? Granted, she'd definitely had more important things on her mind. Like trying not to get eaten herself.

Charlie growled. "We didn't exactly have time for me to cook dinner."

"It's always the assholes that get lucky," Raul muttered.

She dressed quickly, stepping out from the warm tent and quirking a brow at the two men. "You boys done fighting now?"

Raul snorted, rolling his eyes.

Charlie gave her a stiff nod and turned to Raul. "Thank you for the clothes. I appreciate it."

"We appreciate it," Nessie added. "You wouldn't happen to

have any extra tents lying around? Because this one here is toasty warm. What's this shiny material holding all the heat in, anyway?"

Raul pursed his lips, looking away from her for a moment before clearing his throat. "It's a UV-blocking and microwave lining. It keeps me from burning up during the day."

Charlie whistled. "That's some high-tech stuff."

"Yes, it is," Raul said in a clipped tone. "There's an abandoned cabin a few miles north. If you hurry, you can make it there before the sun comes up."

Nessie nodded, screeching as Charlie swept her up again. "Seriously!"

"You heard the man. We have to hurry."

"And I'm too slow. Blah. Blah. Blah." She let her head fall back over his arm, sighing. "Fine. Onward, stallion."

She heard Raul bark in laughter just before Charlie sped off.

The cabin came into view just before dawn, just as Raul predicted. Charlie set Nessie on her feet before creeping through the door and finding it exactly as the stranger said - abandoned. Charlie spotted an electric panel on the side and wondered if the cabin ran on solar power. The cabin was old, at least a hundred years, and whoever had built it had been smart enough to install a wood-burning fireplace. Oil and gas resources had been depleted decades ago after the humans had recklessly ignored warnings from top scientists for over a century. The cabin also must have once been home to a vampire. There wasn't a single window to allow sunlight to filter into the cabin.

Charlie found the breaker box just inside the front door and flipped the main power on. When no lights came to life, he sighed and darted back outside to snatch up some firewood before the sun came up. He set about starting a fire in the mantle while Nessie found some candles in one of the side-table drawers. As soon as he had a flame going, she lit one of the candles and disappeared into another room. He heard a faucet run. The electric must be for a well pump for there to be running water this far into the wilderness.

Nessie came practically skipping into the room with a large metal bucket as the fire crackled to life.

"You seem awfully happy about something," he said.

She smiled over at him, and his breath hitched in his throat. He had never seen her smile like that. Happiness looked radiant on her, and he made a mental note to aim for smiles like that more often. "There's a bathtub, and I am dying to try it out," she chirped.

Images of her nude body luxuriating beneath warm water had him fighting back an erection. "That sounds nice," he replied, keeping his voice as neutral as possible.

"Well, if it's anything close to those hot showers at Dina's..." she moaned, and the sound went straight to his groin, pictures of that nude body he was imagining moaning for more sinful reasons. Her eyes sparkled at him. "It's going to be better than nice."

He smiled back at her even though he really wanted to kiss her senseless...and then some. "In that case, allow me to help." He pulled the small rack from beside the mantle and hooked the pail of water to it, swinging it around to settle above the flames. Given this place had been abandoned for a few decades, he doubted the water heater was still working properly.

An hour, and several heated buckets, later, Nessie disappeared into the bathroom with her tubful of warm water. His acute hearing zoned in on every rustle of clothing, every slap of the water against her skin.

Nessie sighed as the water cocooned her like a warm, gentle blanket. She closed her eyes, allowing herself to relax in a way she hadn't done since...ever. It was heaven, or as close to heaven as she had ever come to. Freedom had some major perks.

The creak of the door had her snapping her eyes open. Charlie stood in the doorway, leaning casually against the doorframe as he watched her. His body language was relaxed, but when her eyes settled on his she found them darkening, giving his thoughts away.

"Not much to do. Do you mind if I sit and talk while you enjoy your bath?" he asked.

She should say no, especially with the obvious state of arousal emanating from his increasingly-dark eyes. But she found herself nodding, and he stepped into the small room. His gaze flickered down her body beneath the water before he sank down to the floor, his back against the door.

"How long until you need to feed?" It had been more than a day, and she didn't know how much he had actually ingested in his attack on Jaxon.

His jaw ticked slightly as his mouth pressed into a hard line. "A few hours, maybe."

She bit her bottom lip, worrying what would happen when the time came for him to feed again.

She heard him sigh and she looked over at him, finding his eyes no longer dark, but stormy blue once more. "Don't worry, Nessie. I can survive on animal blood if need be. I will just be considerably weakened."

His answer brought her the reassurance that he would not feed from her if she did not allow him to. "Animal blood weakens you?"

He nodded.

"How much?"

"I will be no match for other vampires, even those younger than myself."

So, animal blood would compromise his ability to protect himself...and her, for that matter. "And lycans?"

"Not if they're in animal form. In human form, I may stand a chance."

Severely compromised then. But she pushed that thought aside. "Does animal blood taste different?" she asked, curious. She wondered if it was like the way chicken tasted different than beef.

Charlie nodded, but didn't offer any explanation. Fine, she'd have to pry it out of him.

"Better or worse?"

His eyebrow quirked at her curiosity. "Animal blood is like humans eating rotten food compared to eating a fresh meal."

Nessie wrinkled her nose in disgust. She certainly wouldn't want to eat rotten food unless absolutely necessary. "Do all humans taste the same?"

His mouth twitched into a tiny smile for a moment as he stared at his hands. "Not even close."

Again, he didn't elaborate, and the question she wanted to ask got lodged in her throat out of embarrassment. She didn't need to know. Really, she didn't. "What do I taste like?"

His gaze snapped up to hers, studying her for a moment. "Are you sure you want to know?"

He was afraid she wouldn't like what she heard. She was afraid of that too. Damn her curiosity. "Yes, I'm sure."

"I've tasted thousands; and none of them, not one, holds a candle to you." She watched as his eyes tinted from blue to purple. "It's like wine and whiskey blended to perfection." Her breath quickened as he bit his bottom lip with a fang, his eyes turning deep red. "Addictively sweet with a bite that leaves you wanting more."

That should have disgusted her. But her heart pounded for a different reason. She sounded delicious. And from the looks of him, he wanted another taste.

"What stopped you from draining me?"

He was still worrying his lip with his fang, and he really needed to stop. It was making her brain go fuzzy. "I would never hurt you."

She rolled her eyes. "Yeah, because being chomped on by a full-grown man isn't painful at all." Okay, so it hadn't hurt that bad. His little nip back at the mansion was peachy compared to the other vampires. But still...

He frowned. "I tried to be as gentle as possible, but I didn't want to force pleasure on you when you were obviously uncomfortable with the whole thing."

"Force pleasure?" she asked, blinking at him. "On me? Only vampires get pleasure from feedings."

His frown flipped into a smile that matched the smoldering look in his eyes, now a few shades darker. "Not at all. Feedings can be very pleasurable for both giver and receiver."

She didn't believe him. She didn't. An image of her mother popped into her head, pleasure all over her face as Master fed from her throat. "How?"

His tongue flicked over the tips of his fang then slid across his lip, his eyes a deep, dark crimson. And her stomach fluttered, heat blooming low in her belly. Gods, why did she find his fangs so attractive? "There's a gland on the roof of our mouth we can press with our tongue. It shoots a hormone that induces pleasure into the fangs. Then, when we feed, the giver's pain is blocked out by pleasure."

Her jaw fell open, her eyes darting over his face. Silent minutes ticked by as they stared at each other. His gaze flickered to her throat as she swallowed hard.

"Show me," she said.

CHAPTER FIFTEEN

His eyes jumped back to hers. "What?" He saw an array of emotions - determination, curiosity, and...was that lust he saw lingering in the depths of her eyes? He studied her for another moment, sure he'd gotten that last part wrong, but no. It was there.

The water slushed around as she stood, droplets of water sliding down her skin. He watched, awed and surely black-eyed by now, wanting to follow each droplet with his tongue.

"I said show me," she replied, a layer of heat in her voice. He could hear the slight quickening of her heartbeat as her eyes drilled into his.

The candles in the room illuminated her curves perfectly, and he eyed her with greed, watching her gracefully step out of the tub. She snatched her oversized sweater from the sink and threw it over her head. Damned clothing had to ruin everything.

He stood, his body hardening as she approached him. Even though he'd been needing this since the day they'd escaped the mansion, he wanted to be absolutely positive she knew what she was asking of him. "Show you?" he asked.

She nodded. "Yeah. Show me how your fangs can give me pleasure instead of pain."

"You...you want me to bite you?" His entire body coiled like a snake ready to strike.

"Yes." There was no mistaking the lust billowing from her body like a heady perfume and his cock responded in kind. She held her wrist out for him, and he smirked at her. Oh, she thought it would be so simple. Think again, baby.

"Follow me," he said, taking her offered hand in his.

Confusion flitted across her face as he pulled her from the small bathroom. "What? You can't bite me in there?"

He stopped in front of the fireplace and turned to face her. "I wanted to make sure you were comfortable first."

She rolled her eyes, shoving her wrist at him again. "I'm comfortable. Now, get on with it."

His lips curved in a devious grin. "If you insist."

Grabbing her offered arm, he pulled her against him. He lowered his head to run lips along the side of her neck. She jumped in surprise but didn't push him away. Skimming his lips over her shoulder, he grazed his fingers over her peaked nipple through the sweater. He was rewarded with a feminine gasp. He made a quick decision to take advantage of her open mouth, tangling his tongue with hers. Her tongue slid over his fangs, pleasure shooting straight to his groin. The scent of her arousal floated up to him, making his mind fog with lust. He wanted everything, anything she was willing to give. He kept his lower half in check, throwing his desire into the heated kiss.

"I said show me how your fangs can give me pleasure, not your mouth," she murmured as she broke the kiss, her tone husky and breathless.

"Fangs, mouth, same general area," he muttered and dove back into her delectable mouth. She kissed him back for a moment before breaking away again.

Her heavy-lidded eyes hardened. "You lied to me, didn't you?"

That she didn't believe him made him want to scream. "No, I didn't."

If she wanted some fang action, then that was exactly what she would get. With a few tweaks, of course. He tugged her back, lifting her as he took a seat on the couch behind him. With her thighs straddling his, her core brushed over his erection still trapped within his jeans. Damned clothes had to ruin everything!

They both sucked in a sharp breath as he moved his mouth down her jaw, sliding the tips of his fangs over the delicate column of her throat. He pressed his tongue to the gland, his fangs lengthening in response to the hormones pouring into them. It made him crave more than just her blood.

Her hands came up, fingers gliding through his hair as she held his head at her throat in a silent plea. She wanted this. Her body was lighting up for him. He smiled against her throat. *Mine*, he thought as he sank his fangs into the perfection of her skin. She cried softly, pleasure and surprise in her voice.

Her blood poured into his mouth, turning his cock to steel, and the hormones worked their magic. She clung to him, their bodies flush, chest to chest, groin to groin. When she started rocking against him, he nearly came undone right there. Her core slid over the material covering his erection, sweet, sharp pleasure with every movement.

His hands slid up her thighs, finding her bare beneath the sweater. In that moment, it took everything he had not to tear the pesky jeans off himself so he could feel her, wet and warm as she slid over him.

He took one more gentle pull from her throat, then withdrew his fangs and slid his tongue over the pricks to close the punctures.

This is amazing. Nessie felt Charlie's tongue slide over the hypersensitive skin at her throat. It seemed her entire body had been electrified, sparks of pleasure setting her on fire. Charlie's mouth slid up her neck and jaw, finding her mouth and taking possession of it. She rocked against him as her tongue flicked the tip of his fang, drawing a strangled moan from him. She smiled against his mouth. So, fangs were an erogenous zone for him. Good to know.

She did it again. And again. Torturing him with pleasure. His fingers tightened on her hips momentarily before gliding beneath her sweater. She gasped as his fingers rasped over her nipples. She tightened her grip on his hair, pulling gently. A low growl of approval drifted from his throat, and her body flushed with liquid heat in response to the primal, masculine sound.

In a moment, she found herself with her back pressed into the cushions beneath her. Charlie loomed over her, his larger frame pressing into hers. Her legs instinctively wrapped around his waist, and he rubbed himself against her most sensitive place.

She cried out, and realized they were both panting. Her body screamed at her, craving more. More what? More pleasure? With the way her body shook with it, she didn't know how that was possible.

Charlie broke the kiss, breathing heavily. She had never heard him sound out of breath before.

"I want to touch you so badly," he croaked, his voice raw and throaty.

"You are touching me," she countered quickly, wanting his mouth on her again.

She caught a hint of a smile before he opened his eyes, the red completely extinguished by pure, black lust. Black is my new favorite color, she thought as her stomach fluttered.

"No," he said, his body pulling away, and she wanted to cry at the loss. But he didn't let her regret the loss long as his fingers skimmed down her torso, making her skin tingle in sweet anticipation. "Like this," he whispered in her ear as his hand found her core, his fingertip brushing lightly over the tiny bundle of nerves.

Oh, my sweet heaven. Fire licked over her skin at the raw, undeniable pleasure making her body tremble. He was watching her, his dark gaze locked with hers as his expert fingers danced over her. Her voice was lost to her as her body shook violently. It was too much. She was going to explode if he didn't stop.

"Too...too much." Her nails sank into his shoulders as he pulled her into another heated kiss. She bit his bottom lip to keep from screaming.

Forever. He needed *this* forever. This feeling. This body. This woman. Forever.

Every instinct in Charlie's body told him to take her. To possess her completely. To mark her as his mate. To bring her into his world completely so this would never have to end. That's what most of his kind did when they found their mates. If they weren't already immortal, that is. The thought of losing her to old age made him clutch her a little tighter.

She was untouched and being the only man to do so floored his libido into a possessive rampage. He checked his need to be inside her by gently pushing a single finger into her warmth. Pulling out of the kiss, he watched as her eyes widened in shock just before her body fragmented in his arms. Her lip bled as she finally released it to let out a strangled, desperate cry. He watched her come apart, her perfect body arching beautifully. He kept one hand on her core, bringing her down from the pleasure high.

Her eyes popped open, flecks of sparkling gold in the hazel. "What...what the hell was that?" she gasped through labored breaths.

He waggled his eyebrows. Okay, ego check. But he couldn't get the smile off his face. "Oh, I think you know."

Her eyes narrowed on him just before she scrambled off him. "What did you do to me?" Fear edged into her voice, making him stand to comfort her, but she backed away, warning him off as her gaze dropped to his groin where his raging hard-on pointed straight at her. Her eyes widened for a moment before flickering back up to his.

"You asked for pleasure," he said. And, oh man, did he deliver.

Her jaw ticked as she clenched her teeth. "From your fangs, I said."

"I used those too, didn't I?"

She closed her eyes as she inhaled deeply. "What did you do to me?"

What kind of a stupid question was that? "I gave you an orgasm," he said, taking a step toward her and holding out his hand. She held her ground this time, watching him warily as her eyes dropped to his hand, which was coated with the evidence of what he'd done to her.

Her body still trembled and realization dawned on him. He knew she had been untouched by another male, and from the fear and confusion that shadowed her face, she had never sought self-gratification either. He made her orgasm for the first time.

Ever. Gods, that was not going to help his hard-on problem.

CHAPTER SIXTEEN

CHARLIE SAW HER EYES WIDEN IN RECOGNITION. SHE KNEW the word, that was obvious as her cheeks flushed and her kiss-swollen lips parted in surprise, making him want to kiss her senseless all over again. He took another step toward her. Her wide eyes darted down his body again, but she didn't move away from him. As he reached his hand up towards her face, her body stiffened in a silent message: No.

He sighed and dropped his hand to his side.

"I didn't ask you to do that," she snapped at him, her arms wrapping around her body

He stepped away from her, needing distance from her stinging rejection. "You didn't tell me to stop, and neither did your body."

"And that gives you the right to violate me?" Her voice rose with anger.

His molars ground at the insult, his own frustration moving his body forward, stepping into the space he had just created between them. "Let us get one thing clear, Vanessa." She bristled at the name, but he didn't care. "What just happened, we both wanted. And don't deny it because we both know it's true," he snapped as he saw her open her mouth in an attempt to rebut his claim. "You wanted me to bite you, to prove to you that it can be pleasurable. I'm over four centuries old. I know when a woman wants me. And you I happen to be particularly in tune with. You wanted me five minutes ago. Fangs and all. So, stop acting like now they're suddenly a problem."

She closed the distance between them, anger radiating from her as she got in his face. "They are a problem. Vampires have ruined my life, and you were one of them!"

"How in the fuck did I ruin your life?"

Her face reddened as she clenched her fists, eyes shimmering with tears. "You left!"

He sucked in a shaky breath at her words, shame dousing the flames of his fury.

"You were supposed to be my friend. My best friend. My only friend. And you just...left. No goodbye. No 'I'll be back' or 'I'll miss you.' Just...nothing." The tears slid from her eyes, sparkling like yellow diamonds. She blinked, more tears overflowing as she sniffled and took a calming breath. When she looked back at him, the anger was gone. Only a deep, raw pain caught his gaze. "Ten years, Charlie. You left me in that god-forsaken mansion for ten years. Now, all of a sudden, you're back and you expect me to just fall into your waiting arms?"

His shoulder slumped as she threw his biggest regret in his face. "I can't change the past, Nessie. As much as I wish I could go back and save you from it all, I can't. I left because Jacques ordered me to. If I hadn't obeyed him, he would have suspected I was working against him. I had to leave."

She studied him for a moment, crossing her arms over her chest. "You didn't mind disobeying him to save me now. What changed over the last decade?"

"You didn't leave me much choice. Jacques would have killed you."

"He could have done that at any time during the decade you were gone. You weren't too worried about it then."

He had no clue what she would mean to him when he left all those years ago. His heart had been dead and cold, and hell-bent on his vengeful plans. Her blood had broken the icy walls he'd built over the centuries, her wit and determination thawing him out and making him crave a happiness he'd never known. Her gaze a beacon of hope. Her touch calling him home. And he knew she felt the connection. Even if she didn't understand what it meant. So, why was she clinging to the past?

Well, he knew all about clinging to the past, didn't he?

"Jacques murdered my parents."

She blinked at him. "What?"

"In the 1860's, he came to my family's house."

"Why didn't he kill you?"

"My father made me hide in the crawlspace beneath the house. Their blood spilled through the cracks in the floor and covered me and my scent."

"So...you survived and then what? Decided it looked like fun and joined him?"

He wrinkled his nose. "What the fuck? Of course not!"

She swiped at her damp face. "Then why have you been his lap dog for however long you've been following him around?"

"Revenge," he said, pursing his lips. "I let him turn me because it was the only way I could kill him. I couldn't change what happened to my parents. And I can't change what happened to you," he said, wanting to pull her into his arms and stop her tears. "All I can do is make it up to you now. I got you out of the mansion, gave up on my plans for taking Jacques out. Plans I've been working on for centuries. For you."

There was a long silence as they stared at each other before Nessie finally stepped back, shaking her head at him. "You should've done that ten years ago."

With that, she turned on her heel and ran into the bathroom, slamming the door behind her. But the door didn't stop the soft sounds of her sobbing from reaching him, making him realize that he'd broken her heart without knowing it. And he needed to find a way back into it.

"Nessie," a distant voice called. A gentle hand brushed across her cheek as she heard it call again. "Nessie, wake up."

She groaned and peeled her heavy lids open. Charlie crouched beside her, his hand still on her face.

"It's time to get going, Ness. The sun's going to set any minute."

She wrinkled her nose and buried her face in the crook of her arm.

He chuckled. "If you don't wake up, I will be forced to find more creative ways to entice you."

Peeking out from her arm, she glared at him. "Don't you dare," she growled, her voice muffled by the soft material of her sweater. His scent was all over it, and her dreams had taken their lusty encounter to a whole new level. She should shred this sweater...but it was the only one she had.

"Alright, I warned you," he said, coming towards her.

"Fine, I'm up." She rose from the couch she'd crashed on after he'd offered her some cooked rabbit meat he'd made for her. Damn his sweetness. She'd accepted the meal without hesitation. Damn her stomach. She crossed the room and found her other belongings where she'd left them.

As soon as she opened the door to step outside, she knew this was going to be a long night. The wind bit at her exposed skin, and her nose and cheeks would be red and numb within a few minutes. Charlie stepped up behind her. She could feel his body graze her back and her body warmed. Traitorous body of hers always wanting the one person she did *not* want. She stepped away and started trekking forward.

Charlie fell into step beside her, and she glanced over at him. If the cold bothered him, he wasn't showing it. They walked in silence and she didn't glance his way again.

A light snow started soon after, but it didn't stay that way long. The wind picked up, threatening to throw her off balance, and the snow slapped at her face as she tried to press forward. As much as she tried, she couldn't stop her teeth from chattering and her body from shaking beneath the thick sweater and boots she wore.

She halted when Charlie's fingers grasped her arm, pulling her to a stop. "Can you continue in this?"

She simply nodded in answer, afraid her voice would be lost in the wind anyway.

"Are you sure?"

Nessie rolled her eyes and pulled her arm from his grasp, continuing forward.

As much as she wanted to deny it, her steps were beginning to slow, and pushing against the wind was draining her fast. She held on, refusing to let the weakness stop her. Her body was almost numb and taking a breath of the cold air felt like icy spikes.

She stumbled on her feet but caught herself. Another few steps. Stumble. Another step. When she lost her footing the third time, Charlie's arms wrapped around her.

He came in front of her, one arm holding her up while the other stripped his shirt off and pulled it over her shoulders. When he lifted her into his arms, cradling her against his body, she shook her head violently. Being this close to him was dangerous, especially in her fragile state.

He glared down at her. "You can barely put one foot in front of the other and your lips are blue."

"I...I...I'm......f...fi...fine," she stuttered through chattering teeth.

He shook his head at her as he turned around and began walking back the direction they came. "Sure you are."

"R...r...real...really."

"We've barely been out in this for an hour, and I don't know how long until we come across some kind of shelter. We are better off turning around and going back to the cabin until this blows over."

"I...I...c...can...walk...my...myself."

He smirked. "You can barely talk, let alone walk all the way back." He smiled down at her. "Besides, I don't mind carrying you."

Had her cheeks not already been red from the cold, she would have blushed. She did feel herself smile, tried to stop it, and failed miserably.

His smile widened before his eyes went back to the path of tracks that marked their way.

The journey back to the cabin took half the time with the wind pushing them forward. He kicked the door open and deposited her on the small couch before disappearing outside again.

Nessie huddled inside the layers of clothes, cupping her face with her hands in an attempt to warm her bitter cheeks and nose. Charlie returned a few minutes later with a bundle of wood in his arms. He kicked the door shut and dropped the bundle next to the fireplace.

Nessie sighed as the flame sparked and the fire started crackling. She closed her eyes at the beautiful sound, waiting for the heat to reach her.

Suddenly, his shirt was pulled off her and she opened her eyes. Charlie started pulling her sweater off her.

Nessie yanked the sweater closer to her. "What are you doing?"

His eyes found hers, sadness in the blue depths. "I'm sorry, Ness, but I can't risk losing you to hypothermia. Your lips are still blue. You need to take these wet clothes off and get in front of the fire with me."

Her eyes widened. "I need to what? I don't think so." She shook her head, trying to back away. Charlie. No clothes. Bad idea. Dangerous idea. Even the thought was dangerous.

He closed his eyes, shaking his head. "I refuse to let you die because of stubbornness. You need to get direct heat on your body. The wet clothes are in the way. Either take them off or I will."

Her jaw clenched as she narrowed her eyes at him. "I've already had one bastard strip me, so..."

She saw his jaw tick in response. "This is not the same, and you know it. Those wet clothes need to come off."

He moved his hand towards her, and she smacked it away as she glared death at him. "I can do it myself."

He nodded and turned away from her. At least he was giving her some privacy. She peeled out of her sweater, already feeling more heat from the fire without the wet garment covering her skin. She glared at the back of Charlie's head, hating that the man was always right. When she saw Charlie beginning to strip his own drenched clothes off, heat flushed her cheeks and she turned away herself. She didn't want to see him naked. Not. One.

Bit.

"Step toward the fire," Charlie whispered next to her ear, making her jerk.

She complied, closing her eyes as the heat from the fire seeped into her. Then she felt Charlie step up behind her, his skin coming flush against her back. She stiffened, her skin tingling as warmth radiated from his body into hers. His fingers slid over her hips making her shiver.

"You're freezing. Turn around and face me. I need to make sure your chest stays warm. I don't want your heart giving out."

She didn't move. After a moment, she heard him sigh. "Stubborn woman." His fingers gripped her hips, forcing her body around as her arms came up over her chest. The corner of his mouth lifted in a small grin as he pulled her into him, her breasts flattening against his chest.

She watched his eyes darken as his arms wrapped around her. Don't, don't, don't! Her face must have showed her distress because a moment later he closed his eyes, lowering his head.

"I'm sorry, I can't help it." He opened his eyes, almost completely black now. "You can't blame me for wanting you. You're smart, strong, not to mention beautiful. What man wouldn't?"

Heat rose in her cheeks at his compliment, and she shook her head. "Don't try to butter me up with your sweet talk."

His eyes widened for a moment. "You don't believe me?"

She rolled her eyes.

His hands slid down to her rear, pushing her hips forward as the hard edge of his erection slammed into her pelvis. She gasped, liquid heat pooling between her thighs at the intimate contact.

His black eyes blazed in the firelight. "It would seem my body disagrees with you."

She stared at him, speechless, her mind foggy and slow.

He leaned forward, his breath grazing her shoulder. "Do you believe now?" he whispered into her ear.

There is no way I have hypothermia, she thought. She felt as if she were on fire. "Do I have a choice?"

He pulled back, locking his eyes with hers. "You know I want you."

"Well, that's obvious." She smirked at him. "Not like you hid that well."

"True." His dark eyes bore into her. "And I know you want me."

Her smirk vanished. "I can't help how my body responds."

He shook his head, his fingers gliding over her back. "You and I both know that's a cop out."

She wanted to pull away, but the heat of his body felt too good. "What's a cop out?"

He lowered his head, his lips landing on the tender flesh of her shoulder. She sighed, closing her eyes. Relishing the sweet sensation. Even though she shouldn't. "It's when you're making lame excuses that you know are bullshit."

She shook her head but didn't say a word. His mouth opened as he kissed her skin. She was shaking. She could feel it, but for some reason, she didn't care.

"You want me, Nessie. You know you do."

She shook her head again. His hands moved to her stomach, making the muscles jump in anticipation. She knew what those hands were capable of, and the memory of the pleasure he gave her flooded back, her knees buckling at the thought. He caught her with one hand wrapped around her body. His mouth still locked on her shoulder.

"Say you want me," he demanded, his voice low and full of promise against her skin.

She bit her lip. "I can't." She couldn't say it out loud. She could barely admit it to herself.

The fingers of his one hand slid down her stomach as his other arm held her up, her body weak. His mouth grazed over her shoulder, sending shockwaves of pleasure rippling down her body as he licked and kissed his way up the column of her throat.

"Please, Nessie. I need to hear you say it, just once. Please." His voice cracked with lustful need. The sexy voice she had called it once before. His fingers slid through the soft curls between her thighs as his fangs scraped against her neck. The evidence of her true desires slid down the inside of her leg as her core wept with want.

Tears pooled in her eyes. He was right. He knew she wanted him. She wanted him so badly her whole body wept with it. She wanted his eyes dark and his body hard. She wanted his hands and mouth on her body. She wanted the pleasure she knew he could make her feel. She wanted her fingers in his hair and on his body, torturing him with pleasure as he was torturing her.

"Yes," she croaked.

He froze. "Yes, what?" he asked, pulling his mouth from her skin and lifting his head. His brows furrowed in concern as he caught sight of the tears in her eyes.

She took a breath, staring into the dark depths of his eyes. "Yes, I—-."

"If you wanted to fuck her, all you had to do was ask. I might've let her join us if you asked nicely."

Nessie's heart froze, and her flushed body chilled instantly. She knew that voice. The sneering, cold words rolled through her as she peeked around Charlie and confirmed what she already knew.

CHAPTER SEVENTEEN

NESSIE STEPPED up beside Charlie, grabbing his hand to stop hers from shaking.

"She'd already proven worthy of the gift during her lashing. Just like you did, my boy."

She heard Charlie growling under his breath. Glancing over at him, she was startled to see such hatred in his eyes. "I'm not your boy."

"Obviously not if you'd steal from me like a common thief. I'm here to recover my property."

Charlie pulled her behind him again. "You will not touch her."

Master's smile widened. "Oh, I will, I assure you. But I'm saving that bloodbag for last."

The sun hadn't set long ago. She and Charlie should make a run for it while they could. But all thought of running was forgotten as Master stepped further into the cabin...pulling her mother along with him.

"Mom!" Nessie tried to dart around Charlie, but he shot his arm out to stop her. She ducked underneath, and his arms wrapped around her torso, pulling her back against him. Nessie struggled against him, gaining a few inches before he would yank her back again.

Master's smile faltered as he watched the two of them. Mother's face, riddled with bruises, a broken nose, and several cuts, broke into a smile.

"Stop playing with her," Master called.

"I'm not," Charlie snapped through clenched teeth.

"Nonsense!" Master shouted. "You're not using your full strength for fear of hurting her. You disgust me! Had I known you were such a sappy, weak fool, I never would have turned you!"

"She has more strength than you know, Jack."

"Shut up, Eva!" Master struck her and she fell to the floor.

"Don't you touch her, you bastard!" Nessie yelled as she continued to struggle to get to her mother.

Master's face was in front of her a moment later, fingers closing around her throat. She immediately stopped struggling and Charlie's arms fell away from her a moment later.

Master's grip tightened just before her own hand shot up, her palm slamming into the underside of his chin. Charlie's head popped up behind Master as he grabbed the sides of his head and yanked.

Precious air filled her lungs as Master released her to deal with Charlie. The two moved faster than she could follow, but she could see through the flashes of movement that Charlie was losing the battle. She moved toward them wanting to help, but

Charlie paused long enough to shake his head at her. Master used that small distraction to his advantage and had Charlie kneeling on the floor in front of him a moment later, his arms twisted at an odd angle behind his back.

From his pocket Master pulled a long piece of chain, wrapping it first around Charlie's wrists and then around his ankles, leaving Charlie in an awkward, painful kneeling position on the floor.

Master smiled, an evil grin of triumph. "That should hold you until I'm finished." He turned toward Nessie, who whipped around and fled into the kitchen, but Master caught up with her just as she reached for the knife block. "Quick little minx, aren't you?" He grabbed her by the hair, yanking her back into the other room where Charlie and her mother were still on the floor.

He threw her onto the floor next to Charlie, her skin scraping along the hard floor before she thudded into the wall. When she looked up, Master was hauling her mother to her feet, pulling a dagger and pressing it to her mother's throat. He faced the two of them on the floor, his eyes narrowing. "Either one of you move, and she's dead."

It was no bluff, and they all knew it.

Master scraped the weapon along the column of her mother's neck, her mother standing there calmly as he did so. When he nicked her collar bone, she winced, but only slightly. Master continued to leave small cuts along her exposed skin, but she remained quiet. Nessie was shaking with the urge to move. To hurt. To maim.

Master led her mother over to the couch, having her sit on the far end of it with her hands on the armrest. Then, he slammed the dagger through both hands and into the arm of the chair. Her mother screamed.

"No!" Nessie moved toward her mother.

Master pointed a threatening finger at her. "Don't move or

the dagger will be in her heart instead of her hands," he growled at her.

Nessie stilled, but there was no hiding the murderous glare she was undoubtedly giving him. Because she was picturing him in her mind...only bloodier, with some limbs missing.

Master glanced back at her mother. "Stay put, Eva." Her mother looked up at him through her tears and slowly nodded. He walked right past her, grabbing Charlie and dragging him across the floor by the chain, situating him in the center of the room to face Nessie. Charlie's eyes darted down to Nessie's hands, where she saw her palms bleeding from her nails digging into the skin in her struggle to remain still. His eyes didn't turn red as she would have thought but remained vibrant blue.

Master didn't waste any time with subtleties. A second dagger was pulled from a pocket of his jacket. He sliced it across Charlie's chest, tearing his shirt and revealing a long, oozing cut. "Stop!" she begged, tears welling in her eyes again.

Master ignored her, making a second slice across Charlie's thigh. He jammed the blade into Charlie's stomach, twisting and drawing a painful roar from his victim.

Her skin crawled and her body shook with rage. She was losing control of herself. She had no idea if vampires would die from bleeding out, but she had no intention of finding out with Charlie as the potential pile of ash.

When Master slashed an X over Charlie's heart, something within her snapped. Remaining on the floor was no longer an option. She would not allow Master to pierce Charlie's heart with that dagger. A strange surge of energy coursed through her as her gaze locked onto her target.

Nessie sprang from the floor, her body crashing into Jacques almost faster than he could track her. He shook his head to clear the pain away and concentrate on the scene before him. A deep, threatening growl reached his ears as Nessie landed on top of Jacques, her small fingers wrapping around his neck and squeezing.

"Do not touch him," she roared, her voice contorted into a low, foreboding bellow. "He is *mine*."

Charlie sucked in a breath as he heard her strange voice utter those words. She'd...claimed him. But as her what?

Then, he witnessed Nessie go from bare, beautiful woman to...oh, my gods....

Fur covered her body and her ears lengthened into sharp points. Her face contorted, the bridge of her nose wrinkling and her cheekbones stretching outward. He watched in awe as Nessie's eyes suddenly shifted. No longer the warm hazel he had gazed lovingly into a mere ten minutes ago. The flecks of gold sparkled brighter, spreading across her iris like dazzling fireworks. Crouching on her four newfound legs, hackles raised, she bared her teeth, razor sharp and ready to tear through someone. She growled, a wordless promise of pain.

Jacques had been caught off guard by her speed and agility. From the look on his face, her strength as she attempted to crush his larynx shocked him as well. However, a moment later, he recovered, pushing her off him and sending her flying.

Charlie gasped, sputtering through the pain it caused his injured stomach, as he saw Nessie flip in mid-air and land and sprint at Jacques without missing a beat.

What was going on? Nessie was human. He'd tasted her blood. Delicious as it was, it was still human.

He tracked her again, catching a glimpse of her furry face as she spun, snatching one of Jacques' ankles in her snout and throwing him across the room. Her eyes still shone bright gold in the dimly lit cabin. He glanced over at Eva, finding her smiling and completely unsurprised by the fact that her daughter had just turned into a lycan.

His eyes shifted back to the two fighting, each struggling for the upper hand. Jacques' fist slammed into her chest, sending her crashing into the bathroom door. Crack! The door splintered, and Nessie slumped against the wood. Jacques appeared in front of her, his fingers twisting in her fur as he yanked her up from the floor. He pounded her face, jerking her head to the side. She snarled, snapping her jaws.

Jacques' head snapped back as Nessie nipped a chunk of chin. He stumbled backward, and Nessie rushed forward to take advantage of it. She latched onto his forearm, ripping into it like a wild animal...literally. He lost his footing, landing on the floor with Nessie astride him, still trying to tear his arm off.

Jacques pried her off him, wrestling her into submission and landing several blows to her head. His fists were coming down in a flurry of motion. When Nessie shifted back to human form, Charlie caught Eva's smile fading.

Charlie squirmed, trying to break the chains that bound his wrists to his ankles. They didn't budge. Charlie's eyes burned with the struggle to remain upright. To not give in to the pain emanating from his abdomen. Her tiny human body flailed haphazardly in an attempt to stop the lethal blows to her body. Her eyes began to flutter, her movements becoming more and more sluggish.

"Nessie! No!" he and Eva said in unison.

"Stop! Please, I'll do anything!" he cried. But it seemed Jacques was too lost in a haze of violent rage to hear him.

Shit, shit, shit, he thought as he realized his only option. He could only hope those few drops of his blood she'd gotten into her system would be enough.

He bent his head, muttering softly to avoid Jacques'

attention. "Blood of my blood, I command you. Defy death and rise again."

The sound of Nessie's grunts faded away. He lifted his head, finding Nessie's eyes closed and her body limp. Jacques, his face still contorted in rage, continued his assault on her unconscious body until even the small movements of her shallow breathing finally ceased.

CHAPTER EIGHTEEN

CHARLIE BENT OVER, PRESSING HIS FOREHEAD ON THE COLD floor as his eyes stung. For the first time in over four centuries, tears streamed from his eyes and sobs tore through his chest. He had witnessed her birth, and now, her death. The pain of his stomach wound faded away as his heart cracked under the weight of his grief. He'd no sooner found her again, and he'd lost her. To the same malicious bastard he had lost every other person he'd ever loved.

He raised his tear-soaked eyes, throwing every ounce of hate he had into his stare. "I will watch you die, you son of a bitch. If it's the last thing—"

Jacques hauled him up, forcing his body upright. "You

disgust me," Jacques spat at him. "Shedding tears for a slave."

Charlie glared at him, his tears making his vision blurry. "Come now, Jacques. We both know she was more than that." She was everything. Everything to him. Best friend. Lover. Partner. Destiny. In that moment, with Nessie lying dead no more than ten feet from him, he knew without a doubt that he would've given anything to prevent it. Even allow this heartless bastard to continue existing.

Jacques' lip curled. "It doesn't matter now, does it?" He tossed Charlie aside, turning toward Eva, who sat calmly on the couch. Her soft, brown eyes hovered on Charlie's face, a knowing smile tickling her lips.

"You?" Jacques called, advancing on Eva and yanking the dagger out of her hand. Eva gasped as he pulled her to her feet. "How did you birth a lycana?"

Eva gave him a hard glare. "I don't know."

He slammed a fist across her cheek, sending her head jerking to one side. "Liar! You must've known what she was to be able to hide it from me. What did you do?"

"I did what I had to do," Eva spat at him.

Charlie heard a soft groan and his eyes turned to find Nessie stirring. Relief flooded his body, his heart beating once more at the sight. It had worked. He went to move toward her but was held in place. Damn these chains!

Jacques descended upon Eva, not noticing Nessie's return to the living. He smacked her, yelling demands for more information in between the blows. Eva, however, remained tight-lipped, which only drew more violent blows.

And then, Nessie's stirring body disappeared from the floor. She reappeared behind Jacques, her bare body covered in short, brown fur. She grabbed his collar with clawed hands, ripping him off her mother and throwing him across the room. He fell against the opposite wall, pieces crumbling around him. His gaze widened as he stared at Nessie standing in front of her mother.

"What the?" Jacques stuttered. "You...you're dead. I just killed you."

"Do not touch her again," Nessie growled, her voice distorted as she stood in front of her mother.

"You're dead. How? How are you...alive?" Jacques' eyes snapped over to Charlie, his gaze filled with fury as comprehension dawned on his bruised and beaten face.

Charlie glanced over at Nessie, her eyes fixed on Jacques, the whites of her eyes glazing over red. Her irises a dazzling bright gold.

"This is why I don't allow fucking mates!" Jacques got to his feet. "I gave you life, boy. You owe me your loyalty!"

"My mother gave me life," Charlie said, his hatred in the hard gleam of his gaze. "You gave me death. I owe you the same."

Jacques charged towards him, but before he could reach him, Nessie appeared before him, shielding his body from Jacques' incoming attack.

"Touch him and die," she threatened in that distorted voice. "He is *mine*."

Charlie's eyes snapped to Nessie. That's two times she'd claimed him now.

Jacques bared his fangs, coming right at her. He had a few handfuls of centuries on her. Nessie was freshly-turned. That gave Charlie's old Maker an advantage.

A split second later, Nessie's fingers fisted in his pale hair, forcing his head to one side. Her mouth opened wide as she exposed Jacques' throat. Charlie's breath caught as he saw the mouthful of fangs. Her canines protruded much like his own fangs, but the rest of her teeth had shifted into more razor-sharp fangs instead of remaining human as vampires did. Her mouth looked like it belonged to a wild animal. And it tore through the old vampire like butter.

Blood spurted from the wound and Jacques scratched at her face, pushing her off him. But she was like a dog with a bone, relentless, slashing at him. Darting in and out until she got an opening and latched onto his throat. Her claws slammed into his chest, and a moment later, Jacques' heart was clutched in her hand. She let him slump to the floor, clutching the hole in his chest as her haunting eyes found Charlie's.

And then she knelt in front of him, laying his vengeance at his feet.

Nessie's head thumped, as if cymbals were crashing behind her eyelids. Her eyes fluttered. It was a struggle to open them. The pain intensified as she blinked in a blinding light. Her eyes finally focused, seeing that the blinding light was the flickering flames of the fire in the hearth. Why did the firelight feel like she was staring into the sun?

"Vanessa?" a booming voice called from behind her. Her hands clamped over her ears as she turned to see who was yelling. Eva shuffled toward her, her hand reaching out to brush a piece of hair from her face. "Are you alright, honey?" her mother's screechy voice echoed, making her wince.

"Why are you yelling? I'm right here," she snapped, clamping her hands over her ears.

Her mother glanced beside her, where she saw Charlie kneeling on the floor. Still in chains. In front of him lie...a heart. Still pumping on the floor. Her gut clenched at the sight.

And there, lying amid a large puddle of blood, was Master. His eyes were a black void, wide and unblinking. Claw marks streaked across his face. Several patches of hair missing, and her stomach churned as she realized his head had been nearly gnawed off.

A rush of emotion filled her chest at the awesome spectacle of sweet karma as the scene reminded her of her father's brutal murder. As she reached out to assure herself that the monster was truly dead, her eyes locked onto her hand...which was completely covered in blood. Her breath hitched as she realized barely an inch of her naked body wasn't splotched with it. She glanced at Charlie, who had only been a few feet from the body. Charlie...who was still chained up.

Had she done this? Had she killed Master? She glanced around for a weapon but couldn't locate one. With her bare hands? How? A human was no match for a vampire, especially one as old as Master.

Emotions flared again as her attention turned to the oddly pleasing taste in her mouth. Terror. Disgust. Relief. Guilt. She didn't know what she felt. *It's a toss-up when you wake up covered in blood and loving the taste of it.*

Her gaze snapped back to Charlie. His big, blue eyes focusing on her as his throat moved. A wave of lust washed over her as her gums began throbbing.

She sucked in a breath as comprehension struck her. The oddly pleasing taste in her mouth; Master's body missing quite a few pints of blood; his throat almost gnawed clean off; the fact that a faint glow of firelight was killing her corneas. Her eyes narrowed on Charlie as Eva knelt to undo the chains. "You bastard," she snarled, rushing towards him. Ready to detach *his* head.

Her mother stepped in front of her, halting her.

"He saved your life, Vanessa." Her mother glared at her.

"I didn't fucking asked to be saved!" she roared, giving Charlie a look that could kill. Being turned into a monster wasn't her idea of being "saved." More like being cursed for all eternity.

Eva rolled her eyes. "Stop being so dramatic. You're alive and that's what matters." She pulled Nessie into a tight embrace. Nessie stiffened as the scent of Eva's blood, which still dripped from the wound in her hand, bombarded her senses. "Thank you, Charlie," Eva murmured against her skin.

Charlie nodded his head while she yanked from her mother's grip. "Typical vampire! I give you an inch and you take my fucking mortality away," she snapped, crossing her arms over her chest. How dare he turn her. He should've known she'd never want this. To be like...Master. Like Logan. Like all of them.

"How could you do this to me?!" Hot tears stung her sensitive eyes, making her scream. "I thought you cared about me!"

"He saved your life," her mother repeated, stroking her cheek with her good hand.

"He should've let me die then! At least then I wouldn't be a monster!"

Her mother pressed her lips together, her eyes darting over to Charlie. An odd look passed between them, as if they knew something she didn't.

"We can't always choose our fate. You have been given a second chance at life. You should start thinking about how you want to use it."

Making the rest of Charlie's life hell sounded like a good plan right now.

CHAPTER NINETEEN

T HE LAST RAYS OF SUNLIGHT VANISHED BEHIND THE DISTANT mountains by the time the three of them washed all the blood off. Charlie poured a bucket of water into the hearth, dousing the flames. And the ashes that were all that remained of Jacques, and the last four hundred years of his life. He stared into the smoke, wondering when he'd feel the weight of his revenge lift. When the happiness he'd been imagining for this moment would wash over him.

He healed Eva's wound on her hand, albeit awkwardly, then she packed some canned goods she found in the cupboards in a makeshift pack she made from the rug. She patted Charlie on the back. "She'll come around. Whether she wants to admit it or not, she's happy she's alive. Even if she's not happy about the circumstances. She'll realize what you've done for her eventually." She gave him a reassuring smile and limped out the door. Because some of her injuries weren't so easily healed.

Nessie came barreling out of the bathroom a few minutes later, fully clothed and refusing to look at him as she stomped past him.

He frowned, sighing as he closed the door on his past and took a shaky first step into the unknown future ahead of him. His gaze was continually drawn back to Nessie, the mate who hated him. The only person in the whole world he wanted in his life. And she couldn't even look at him.

Then, Nessie vanished.   Eva was still trudging along ahead of them, unaware that Nessie was no longer following her. He wondered for a moment if he should carry Eva given her injuries. Even with Jacques gone, there were still plenty of others that could come after them.

Glancing around, he spotted Nessie in the distance, flinging her arms in the air. He sped over to her, hearing her growl.

"I'm fine!" she snapped, walking back towards Eva.

"Your body can go much faster now. It will take time for you to adjust," he said. Because she needed someone to help her with her new abilities. And like it or not, he was her only option.

"I said I'm fine."

He laid a hand gently on her arm. "I expect you to have questions. I am here to help however I can."

She yanked her arm from his grasp, her eyes glowering at him. "You've helped enough, I'd say." She turned and began trekking back to her mother, her speed once again getting away from her as she stopped a few hundred feet further behind Eva and had to backtrack to her.

But before she could get a taste of whatever sweetness lie under her mother's skin, somebody yanked her from her mother's embrace, pulling her further and further away from the source of her sweet treat.

She flailed, fighting against the arms entrapping her as they carried her off.

No! The voice inside her head screamed. *Blood! Blood!*

She turned in his arms, faintly registering Charlie's face, mouth open wide as she prepared to strike.

He dodged, avoiding her fangs. She snapped at him again and again, but he was too fast.

"Calm down, Ness," Charlie grunted in between dodges. He continued to talk to her as she raged against him, sometimes stern, sometimes soothing. Eventually, his voice permeated the red haze that had shrouded her mind from reason and her attack ceased.

Her body slumped against him, going still. Even her breathing stopped. She didn't feel out of breath, but her body was suddenly exhausted beyond comprehension. Where had all that energy gone? Was it the threat of dawn draining her?

She somehow found the strength to lift her head from Charlie's shoulder. "What's happening to me?" She felt as if her new body, with all its abilities, had taken complete control of her. Was this to be her life now? An endless battle with herself? A struggle against her new uncontrollable impulses?

"You need to feed." Charlie told her.

Nessie shook her head furiously. No way. Gross.

"The longer you wait, the more violent and frequent these hunger rages will become. Your body will get what it needs, even if it has to sabotage your mind to do it."

Nessie let her head fall back, groaning. So, trying to sink her teeth - scratch that, her fangs - into everyone in sight was a common   occurrence   when   you   were   a   bloodthirsty vampire. Great. She glared up at Charlie. "You just love making my life hell, don't you?"

Charlie frowned. "I've been trying to keep you alive long enough to escape and truly be free. Unfortunately, freedom is hard to come by in this world, especially for humans."

Nessie huffed. "Well, I'm not human anymore. You saw to that."

His jaw ticked as his eyes grew sad. "I can't deny that I turned you to save your life. In all honesty, it was selfish of me to turn you. I couldn't bear the thought of losing you when I had finally found you."

Nessie wanted to snap at him, but his words gave her pause. He admitted he turned her out of a selfish desire to keep her in his life. "You haven't just found me. You've known me as long as I can remember. And you didn't mind letting me go all those years ago."

Charlie nodded. "If I had known then what I know now, I would have made very different choices. I've only come to realize how much you mean to me since I got back from the council. It felt like I had no time at all with you. I wasn't ready to let you go so quickly."

"Well, isn't this a touching moment," came a snide, male voice.

Charlie whipped around, planting himself in front of Nessie and cursing himself as he saw Eva clutched in the grip of a young male. He'd forgotten that Eva had been leading the trek while he'd been preoccupied with Nessie.

The young male's light brown waves and hazel gold eyes matched an older male behind him to a tee. No doubt the two were related. He eyed them warily. Because humans didn't just wander around these woods alone.

Nessie stepped around him, giving him a nasty look before she turned her attention on the newcomers.

And the older male seemed extremely interested in her. Both females, actually. *Fuck me. Not this again.*

"Torin," the older male stated, authority oozing from his mouth. The younger one turned to look at him. "Release her."

Torin's face held shock for a moment before he obeyed. He stepped toward the older man. "But, pop, they're vampires."

The older male nodded toward Eva, who was...smiling at him? "She's human."

Torin rolled his eyes. "Yeah, but they aren't," he said, pointing towards Charlie and herself.

Eva stepped in front of Torin's pointing finger, but her eyes remained on the older male. "The girl is my daughter, just recently turned." The idiot woman was about to get them both killed, and herself back in the slave market.

Charlie tugged on Nessie's arm, trying to get her to run with him. But she pulled her arm away, glaring at him.

Don't touch me, he heard her voice echo in his mind. Relief flooded him. He'd forgotten about this little perk. Turned mates could communicate telepathically. Finally, some luck.

We need to leave. There could be more of them.

Nessie's head snapped over to him, her eyes wide as her mouth fell open. *D...did you just?*

Yes. Welcome to immortality. We need to go. They're lycans.

The older man's eyes narrowed on Charlie, his jaw ticking. "I suppose the male one's responsible for that?"

Eva went right on telling them their life story. What was wrong with her? "Yes. He saved her life from our former master, who ended her human life as we watched in chains. Had he not turned her, she would be gone forever. I am grateful to him."

The man's eyes softened a bit. Well, he didn't look like he

wanted to rip Charlie limb from limb anymore. "It is nearly dawn," he stated. "The two of you should have sought shelter by now."

Charlie felt his own mouth fall open. A lycan...help them? "I'm sure we'll come across something suitable soon."

"Could you help us?" Eva blurted, her eyes locked onto the older male as if she were trying to hypnotize him or something.

"As if we would help a couple of bloodsuckers," Torin snapped, squaring his broad shoulders and sticking his chin in the air.

"Torin," the older man bellowed, his head turning toward the younger male. "Tell me, son, are you Alpha of this pack?"

Torin lowered his head and muttered, "No."

"Do you speak for me or our pack?"

"No."

"Then mind your place and keep your mouth shut."

Torin trudged over to stand behind the Alpha, contempt shining from his eyes as he glared over at the two of them.

"My basement is currently vacant. The two of you are welcome to use it until the sun goes down."

Torin's shocked face probably matched his own. Why was this lycan so keen on helping them? Had to be a trap.

"But pop..." Torin started, but one stern look from the older man had him clamping his lips shut.

Charlie shook his head. "Are you sure there isn't anywhere else? No caves in the area?"

Alpha shook his head. "The closest one is a half day's journey. You'll never make it in time."

Nessie looked up at the sky. And he knew what she was thinking...because he could hear her mumbling within her own mind. The Alpha was right. The sky had lightened during their little encounter, streaks of purple and pink climbing the horizon. Dawn was far too close for comfort.

Nessie stepped forward. "We accept your kind offer."

Nessie, Charlie growled into her mind.

Nessie turned toward him, thinking he'd spoken out loud. "Don't 'Nessie' me. This is the most logical decision, and you know it."

He turned them to face away from the strangers and Eva. "This could be a trap. They are lycans."

"It's either trust them to lead us to safety or risk frying in the sun trying to find shelter ourselves."

"We could go to ground," Charlie retorted.

Nessie took a step back, her body stiffening. Her thoughts scrambling through his own. The thought of being buried alive scared her more than walking in the sun. Her gaze flitted over his face as she shook her head. "No."

Charlie sighed deep. There'd be no changing her mind on this.

Nessie turned to face the wolves again, trying to manage a smile. "Lead the way."

The Alpha returned her smile, then turned toward Torin, nodding. Torin scowled but waved his hand for them to follow. The Alpha waited for each of them to pass by before taking position at the rear.

CHAPTER
TWENTY

C HARLIE DID NOT LIKE THIS SITUATION. NOT ONE BIT.
   Walking straight into a lycan village was beyond a bad
   idea. It was practically suicide. Why was Nessie so
eager to trust these mongrels after her last unfortunate
encounter with the beasts? Surely the last Alpha she'd come
across had proven just how barbaric their particular species was.
He kept glancing back toward the older wolf, the Alpha of
whatever new pack they'd come across. That was the trouble
with venturing too far from the cities. The wilderness was wolf
territory. Hundreds of miles of nothing but pack after pack of
lycans, each claiming a different stretch of hunting ground.

The Alpha seemed wary of him. Predictable. Vampires and

lycans were natural enemies, in a constant struggle for power. The power struggle had hit a peak a few centuries earlier as the supernatural population grew enough to threaten the human population, eventually bringing the humans to their knees and into slavery. Since then, the two species had gone their separate ways; the vampires choosing to inhabit the urban cities, while the wolves chose the rural areas. The fact that a vampire - make that two vampires - had ventured so far from the cities was highly unusual. As was a lycan, and an Alpha at that, offering shelter to vampires.

Charlie risked another glance back at the Alpha, who narrowed his eyes on him. What was this wolf up to? As a faint glow came into view between the distant trees, Charlie's body tensed as he sensed dozens of bodies, both lycan and human. In front of him, Nessie froze, her muscles tensing. He glanced down to see her nails elongating into tiny claws. Shit. She also sensed all those blood-filled bodies, and having yet to feed since turning, she could turn ravenous in minutes.

He stepped up behind her, gently grasping her arms as he laid his chin on her shoulder. *Soon, Nessie. Be patient. Trust me.*

Her body shook as she struggled to continue forward, her nostrils flaring. "My throat. It hurts." Her voice was beginning to contort. Another dangerous sign that another hunger rage was coming. Soon.

Tell yourself that you will feed soon. Let your mind calm your body down. He ran his fingers gently over her arms trying to distract her from her hunger.

He heard her inhale deeply, a human's way of stress control. "Don't breathe," he commanded, using his voice this time to make sure she heard him. "It will help if you can't smell the blood as strongly."

Her breath hitched a second later.

"Is everything okay?" The Alpha's deep voice pulled him from his focus on Nessie.

He slipped his hand down Nessie's arm, pulling her hand into his as he turned his face toward the Alpha. "It's Nessie. She hasn't fed, and she's starting to lose control."

The wolf's eyebrows raised. "Are you saying she needs...blood?"

He wanted to roll his eyes at the moronic question, but instead he just nodded. "Yes. And soon." His gaze lifted to the sky for a moment. Damn. "There is not enough time for me to take her hunting before dawn. Do you have any livestock?"

A small sign of disgust crossed the Alpha's face before he nodded and motioned for Torin to continue forward.

The last few hundred yards were the longest of the journey as Charlie struggled to keep Nessie under control. Finally, the village came into sight. Tiny flame-lit lanterns hung outside the door of each house that lined a large pathway that ran towards the center of the village. When the door of one of the houses opened, a woman emerged carrying a large basket full of clothes. Nessie let out a low growl as she shot from his grasp toward the woman.

Charlie darted after her, catching her round the middle as her nails became claws and her fangs erupted in her mouth. Charlie struggled against her strength, puzzled. He had over four centuries on her. He should easily overpower her. Instead, she was gaining ground, inching closer to the woman, who jumped when spotting the two of them. She dropped her basket, anger blanketing her face. "Bloodsuckers," she growled under her breath.

Torin and the Alpha came to stand in front of the woman. "No," the Alpha commanded, halting her advance as she gazed up at him.

"They're vampires, Talon!" she screeched.

Talon turned away from the woman, glancing back at the two

of them to watch Charlie struggle. He looked puzzled, and Charlie could guess why. Nessie's fangs were not those of normal vampires. They were canine fangs, almost identical in every way to a lycan's fangs after shifting into wolf form, only smaller to fit inside a human-size mouth. And the nails of a vampire, while deadly sharp, never grew to such claw-like lengths.

"Livestock!" Charlie shouted at them as he yanked Nessie back against his body. "Now!"

Talon's face grew serious, nodding. "Torin."

Torin took off running, disappearing between the rows of houses before returning a few minutes later with a large pig in his arms. He set the pig down a few yards from where Charlie and Nessie stood. Torin wrinkled his nose and backed away to return to his Alpha's side.

Charlie wrestled Nessie toward the pig as she continued to fight to get to the woman. The unconscious pig lay on the ground and Charlie pulled Nessie's face down. "Nessie, look," he coaxed as he risked releasing a hand from her to slash a gash at the pig's thick neck. Blood oozed from the wound, and Nessie's struggle stopped as she turned toward the pig. Her eyes darted between the pig's bloody gash back to the woman, as if contemplating if the struggle was worth the more-tempting blood of the woman.

"You must drink, Nessie. You will feel better, I promise."

His words seemed to convince her as she latched onto the animal. The pig awoke with a squeal as she sank her teeth into the wound, her throat moving as she gulped. Her claws dug into its belly, holding it in place as she drank deeply. After long moments, she yanked her fangs free on a gasp. Her eyes popped open, no longer gold and glowing. She gazed down at the lifeless creature as she clapped her hand over her blood-stained lips.

"I...I killed it," she murmured, looking up at him. She squinted, trying to shield her eyes with her hand. "It's too bright out here."

"This way," Talon said as he walked past them. Charlie helped Nessie to her feet as they followed Talon toward the center of the village. He led them toward one of the larger houses positioned in front of the large, circular fire pit.

She grimaced. "It burns."

Charlie sped up as he felt his own skin begin to tingle painfully. He spotted the rays of sunlight as they began to trickle through the trees.

Dawn had arrived, and the direct sunlight drained their energy instantly. His legs gave out and Nessie toppled down next to him. He tried to cover Nessie's face, but the sun paralyzed them both. Her cheek burned as a beam of sunlight hit her sensitive skin. It blistered in an instant. Talon grasped his wrist, pulling himself and Nessie the last few feet through the doorway and slamming the door shut.

"Close the blinds, now!" Talon demanded. Several pairs of feet scrambled through the house as Talon continued to drag them across the floor, avoiding any patches of direct sunlight that filtered through the windows. "Open the basement door."

A creak and a grunt later, Talon hoisted them into his arms and carried them inside the second doorway. As the door shut, darkness finally welcomed them. Talon carried them down the stairs, setting them on a large, plush pouf chair.

Talon threw the cushions from the large couch across the room, pulling the frame into a full-size bed. When he was finished, he turned toward Charlie. "Sheets, blankets, and pillows are in the closet," he stated, pointing toward a narrow door in the far corner of the room.

Charlie nodded, his energy slowly returning as he stood and took a tentative step toward him, holding out his hand. "I appreciate everything. You saved both of our lives back there. We are in your debt." Charlie couldn't believe a lycan had saved his life. And his mate's, for that matter. Life with Nessie certainly came with plenty of surprises it would seem.

Talon's eyes darted to the outstretched hand, hesitating only a moment before accepting it, shaking it firmly. "I'll hold you to that, vampire," he said, his eyes locked on Charlie's. Apparently, the Alpha had plans for him. Fucking fabulous.

Talon released his hand and exited the room. Charlie heard the lock click and Talon command that no one enter the room other than himself. He wasn't sure if the command was for their protection or the wolves'.

Charlie set to work gathering the linens from the closet. Nessie groaned, her body beginning to stir to life. The sunburn she'd received was already beginning to heal, which was probably why she hadn't recovered her energy as quickly.

Once the bed was made, he gathered Nessie into his arms. She blinked up at him, her eyes swirling. "Charlie?"

"Shhh," he cooed, laying her on the bed. "We're safe. Rest now. It's been a long night."

And that was an understatement. *Her first night as an immortal and she almost burns in the sun.* Somehow, the fact that she couldn't die of old age didn't ease his worries one bit.

By some miracle, probably because she still hadn't recovered - sun damage took a lot of energy to heal - she decided not to argue and simply drifted back off to sleep.

CHAPTER
TWENTY
ONE

NESSIE AWOKE HOURS LATER WITH THE RIGHT SIDE OF HER face tingling with pain. She ran the tips of her fingers over her cheek stifling a hiss. Her mind raced for an explanation, flashing a scene of Charlie carrying her through the village as she watched the sunrise through the trees. Her eyes flickered over Charlie's face. He still slept, his arms wrapped around her, clutching her tightly against him. Her head lay against his bicep as she gazed up at him, debating whether she should try to move. Her gut clenched as her focus landed on Charlie's throat again. The curve of his broad shoulders had other parts of her body clenching as well. Damn her body and its insatiable needs.

A small lean forward would bring her mouth in direct contact with the skin of his throat. Before she could decide, her body had already made the decision for her, leaning forward the few inches it needed. She breathed in his masculine scent of rain and evergreens and she felt his body tense.

"Nessie?" he whispered as she opened her mouth and sank her fangs into his vein. A moan escaped her as the taste hit her tongue. Better than any food she could remember eating as a human. Better than chocolate. And what could be better than chocolate? Charlie, apparently.

He groaned, his fingers tightening on her body, pulling her flush against him. Heat blossomed as she felt his erection rub against her hipbone. He rolled, pulling her atop him, cradling the back of her head against his throat. She grew moist with desire, her senses overloaded with him. A primal instinct had her rocking against him as he clutched her tighter, his fingers tunneling through her hair. The small tug sent a shockwave rippling through her, and she pulled her fangs from his throat.

"Lick," Charlie commanded.

"What?" she breathed; her mind still hazy.

His fingers still held her head against his throat as his other hand splayed across her behind, pushing her core more firmly against him as she continued to move, causing the most wonderful friction. "The wound," he told her. "Lick it shut."

She obeyed, watching the wounds seal shut as she straightened. With the bloodlust satiated, her mind slowly cleared.

Scrambling off him, she touched a finger to her lips, wanting to gag when the tip came away stained bright crimson.

"Ugh! Did I just drink you?" she cried, wrinkling her nose at the thought.

Yes, and he tasted delicious.

Charlie gazed up at her with eyes still glazed black. Oh, great.

He liked getting bitten.

So do you. Remember?

Oh, right. Flashes of what he'd done with those sinful fangs of his flitted through her mind.

Charlie groaned. *Your thoughts are practically screaming at me. If you're trying to turn me off, it isn't working.*

Nessie's eyes widened, automatically dropping to the obvious bulge in his jeans. Another wave of lust swamped her.

The grin on Charlie's face grew.

Son of a bitch, he could still read her thoughts?!

Yep. Every dirty one of them.

Gah! Well, stop it! This telepathy thing felt so invasive. How the hell do you turn this off?

Even if I knew how, I wouldn't tell you. This is way too much fun.

She glared at him, slamming her hands on her hips. "You're an asshole."

Click! Their heads whipped around, staring up at the door they'd just heard unlock. Charlie cursed as he tried to adjust himself, his erection still obvious.

The door creaked open. "I'm supposed to let you know the sun set a few minutes ago. You're safe now." Torin's voice echoed through the basement.

Nessie sighed in relief as the door slammed shut, but no lock clicked this time.

"Are you kidding me?" Charlie huffed. "He interrupts us to tell us the sun set? We're vampires! We know when it sets!"

Nessie rolled her eyes. Interrupted what? This wasn't going anywhere.

What do you mean? It's my turn now.

She scowled at him. "Your turn for what?"

"I let you bite me, didn't I?" Charlie grinned.

Nessie's mouth fell open before she snapped it shut. She gave a nonchalant shrug. "That was your choice. You could've stopped me. By the way, why the hell did I bite you anyway?" She needed to know so she didn't do it again. *I've got to get a hold of myself.*

"It won't help. You'll do it again," Charlie stated, smirking at her as he rose from the bed. "Face it. You find me irresistible."

Growling in frustration, she stomped up the stairs, deciding she'd rather deal with her mother than him right now. After what he'd done to her, she should find him more than resistible. He should be downright deplorable to her. But instead, she was already craving another bite of him. And another bite *from* him.

Nessie heard the soft voice of her mother down the hallway after searching most of the house.

"She did not ask to be turned," Eva snapped.

"Well, it wouldn't have surprised me. The way she looks at that vampire!" Talon retorted.

She heard the screech of a wooden chair scraping along the floor. "That vampire saved her life! She would be dead if he hadn't turned her!"

"And that is the only reason I haven't cut the bastard's head off."

Nessie knew the Alpha didn't like Charlie much, thinking it was because Charlie was a vampire, but now...it seemed more personal than that. He was talking as if Charlie's connection to her was the only thing keeping his head attached. But what would he care about her for? She was also a vampire, and the two reigning supernaturals did not exactly get along.

"You have no idea what Charlie has sacrificed for her. After her father was murdered---"

"I am her father, Eva. You know it, I know it. I knew it the moment I laid eyes on her."

Nessie gasped, smacking her hand over her mouth to silence the sound. No...it couldn't be true. He couldn't be right.

The Alpha continued. "What happened when you left that

day? You never came back."

"After we had that fight, I went for a walk to clear my head," her mother answered, her voice cracking. "Poachers found me. I hadn't realized I'd wandered so far from the village."

Nessie heard the chairs scraping along the floor and her mother's soft sniffling. Why hadn't her mother denied the Alpha's claim?

"I had a feeling something like that happened, but my father said there was nothing to be done. Maybe if he'd known you were pregnant..." he sighed. "I'm so sorry I wasn't there to protect you. Both of you."

"I shouldn't have left the village alone. It was foolish."

Eva's sobs continued, muffled slightly.

"Does the girl know?" Talon asked.

Nessie scowled and stepped into the room. "I do now, don't I?"

They both snapped their heads and stared at her.

"Nessie, honey. I...I" her mother stammered.

Holding up a hand, Nessie interrupted. "Why didn't you tell me?"

Eva sniffled again. "Your life was hard enough. You loved Paul to pieces. I didn't want to ruin the one loving relationship you had in your life.

"Did Dad know?"

"Yes. I married Paul not long before I delivered you. We were sold together, and he claimed you as his own."

"Was he a good father to her?" Talon asked, drawing Nessie's gaze to his face. To the eyes that resembled her own so much.

The best father she could have asked for, Nessie thought, grinding her teeth. "Yes," she snapped.

"He was very affectionate," her mother answered, looking back at him. "When Nessie was young, I struggled. She looked so much like you...it hurt to be around her sometimes. I was lucky he was there. Nessie grew very fond of him. I dare say, she probably loved him more than she loved me."

Taking a step forward, Nessie's vision started to blur. "You were always leaving! Running off to fuck Master. Of course, I hated you for that. Daddy loved you, and you just shoved it in his face."

Eva's lip trembled and Talon wrapped an arm around her. "Don't talk to your mother like that."

Nessie pointed a finger at him. "Do not even think of telling me what to do. You are not my father. My father died at the hands of the monster she fucked every night."

"I didn't have a choice!" her mother sobbed.

"Fucking hell, I'll murder him," Talon growled from behind her mother.

Eva continued, "I had to protect you, and he could've killed any of us in a moment. You saw that with your own eyes, Nessie. If I refused him, he'd have murdered both of you years ago. It was better for him to stay interested in me than take too much of an interest in you. Especially after we found out what you were."

Nessie stopped breathing. "What do you mean 'what you were'?" She found herself stepping back. "As opposed to what I am...now that Charlie turned me?"

Eva had her hand over her mouth, as if she hadn't meant to let that slip. She shook her head. "You...you're not ready."

"Not ready for what?" she asked.

Talon squeezed her mother's shoulder. "You must've been born like me. One of my kind. We both saw you transform during the hunger rage. I've never witnessed it before. As far as I know, we lycans have a natural immunity to vampire blood, which is why we can't be turned. And you must be close to twenty by now. Well beyond the age we begin transforming on full moons."

"No. She never did." Her mother said between sniffles. She stepped towards Nessie. "Me and your Dad gave you tea with wolfsbane in it." She gave a small smile. "That's why you never liked it. But we had to subdue your abilities. Jack would have killed you the moment he realized you were part lycan."

Nessie shook her head and took another step away from them. "No. No."

"I wish I could have been there for both of you," Talon said. "But I can protect you both now."

"Will your pack allow that?" Eva asked, sounding skeptical. "Given she was turned?"

"She's the Alpha's daughter. Although, I still don't understand how she would have had any abilities at all as a child..."

Nessie had stopped breathing. She felt the warmth of fresh tears slide down her cheeks as she listened to the ugly truth of her life. She was a monster. And, apparently, she had been a monster long before Charlie had turned her. Flashes of her life sped through her mind. Lies. All of it. Talon. The Alpha lycan. Her real father. *Holy, shit. Who the hell am I?*

With that last thought, she ran. She didn't know where she was running to, but she knew it was away from her mother and the monster she'd never call "father."

CHAPTER TWENTY TWO

CHARLIE HAD FINALLY MANAGED TO GET HIS LOWER HALF under control and opened the basement door when Nessie flashed by. She hadn't taken notice to him and he sensed something had upset her. Given her lack of impulse control, he followed her at a distance to make sure she didn't bite someone's head off...literally. And that none of these mutts tried to go after her despite Talon's warning.

A few miles outside the village, in a secluded grove, he watched as she crashed to her knees. She sobbed into her hands, the gut-wrenching, gasping-for-air type. He wanted to go to her. To fold her into his arms and allow his body to absorb her tears and tortured cries. He knew she wouldn't accept her new life easily and watching her now made him second-guess his decision to turn her. Not everyone was cut out for this existence, but he thought Nessie's strength and pig-headedness would lend itself well to transition. As Eva had said the night they had escaped, Nessie was a fighter. She showed it time and time again.

But, as Nessie knelt on the ground, her body heaving through her tears, it seemed something had broken her. Something had finally gotten through her iron skin. And that something had happened sometime after she had left the basement.

"Monster," he heard her mutter in between sobs. "I'm a monster."

Charlie took a silent step toward her. She wasn't taking the turning well. But it was too late to take it back now. He stepped out from the shadows. "You're not a monster, Nessie."

She jumped up, turning to face him in one fluid movement. Her eyes were blood-shot and puffy, her cheeks streaked with tears, but she was still the most beautiful mess he'd ever seen. Misery saturated her face as she shook her head. "I am a monster. And apparently, I've always been a monster. No wonder everyone keeps dying around me. It's me."

He took another step toward her, but she held her hand up to stop him.

"No! Don't come near me! I might hurt you. I couldn't bear it if I killed you, and the way your blood tastes, I might very well drain you of every drop."

He smirked at her, trying to lighten the mood. "So, I taste that good to you, huh?" He wiggled his eyebrows.

She rolled her eyes. "This is not funny, Charlie! I could kill you, you know. Right now."

He took another step toward her, allowing his mind to wander to Nessie's surprising and welcoming wake-up call that evening. Her reaction told him his eyes had darkened at the lusty memory. "Really? You want another taste already? Well, I'm game if you are."

He was close to her now, a few arm-lengths and he could pull her against him and make her forget she ever thought she was anything but amazing.

"You don't understand," she cried. "I'm not...I don't even...Oh, gods!" Her hands came up to cover her face as she began sobbing again.

He took the last few steps and pulled her toward him, but she shoved him off.

"Don't! Don't touch me!"

"Nessie, please. You're hurting. Let me help you."

"You can't help me!" she cried, flinging her arms. "There's no helping me out of this, Charlie. I'm a monster, and there's no changing that."

Charlie dropped his outstretched arm. "You're never going to forgive me for turning you, are you?"

"I don't know! Can I have more than 24 hours to decide if I'm okay with it?" she snapped, turning away from him. "And it turns out it's not entirely your fault I'm a monster, anyway."

His hand froze mid-air. She knew? Her mother must've spilled the beans.

She turned her head, her eyes a slightly brighter shade of brown as the gold flecks became more prominent. "According to my mother and... the Alpha," she ground out. "I was never exactly human to begin with." She sighed. "My dad...he wasn't my biological father."

He remembered Paul rushing to Eva's side during Nessie's birth. Only a few weeks after Jacques had bought the pair of them. Though, he still didn't understand how Nessie had been anything but human. He'd had more than one taste of her and never detected anything. Never witnessed any supernatural abilities when she was young. But after yesterday, he'd assumed

Paul couldn't have been the other half of Nessie's gene pool. Two humans couldn't produce...

"Oh, my gods. It's the Alpha." That explained the Alpha's keen interest in the two women when they first crossed paths.

His gaze snapped back to her as she fell to her knees, her hands covering her face as he heard her weep again. "Who am I?"

He knelt next to her. "Your ancestry doesn't change who you are, Nessie."

"Yes, it does! I thought I was human...a plain, human girl who just wanted freedom from all these monsters! Now, it turns out I was one of those monsters all along. And now...now, I don't even know what I am!"

Charlie wanted to comfort her. Reassure her that she was still the same person, but she was right. She wasn't the same. And even he didn't know what she was. Nothing like this had ever happened before to his knowledge. The supernatural species didn't mix. Vampires couldn't procreate, and lycans were immune to vampirism. So, how had it happened with Nessie? If she was born a lycan, how had he been able to turn her? It shouldn't have been possible.

"I should leave. Before I hurt someone. I almost bit my own mother this morning. Who knows what I'm capable of now?"

Charlie sighed. "I don't know if that's the best option right now. Where will you go? The human colonies wouldn't let you anywhere near them."

During his endless meetings with the Ancient Council over the past decade, the colonies had come into the conversation more than once. There weren't many places left on earth for humans to live free of supernatural oppression. The final groups of human rebels had retreated to the poles a few centuries earlier, where the endless summer days made it nearly impossible for a vampire to venture. Not to mention, the humans began focusing all their technological efforts towards keeping the monsters of the world out of their safe haven. He and Nessie wouldn't stand a chance of seeking refuge there.

The harsh reality was that there were even fewer places for rogue supernaturals to escape to. The wilderness was lycan territory. The cities were vampire territory.

"I'll just have to fend for myself from now on, I suppose. Given what I am, I'm assuming I'm at least capable of that."

"You may be stronger, but you are still young, Nessie. There will be plenty of much older vampires...and lycans for that matter, that will be much more experienced than you are. Not to mention if you run into a group of them. No one is invincible."

Nessie lifted her chin. "I killed Master easily enough."

"That was because he wasn't expecting you to turn, much less as...well, whatever you are. You caught him off-guard." He had to convince her because venturing out on her own could be suicide.

"Well, what do you expect me to do? I'm not staying here; I don't care what Talon says."

"Talon offered you to stay with the pack?"

"Yeah. He said that given that I'm technically one of their kind, the pack couldn't refuse me."

"Your safest bet would be to accept Talon's offer. The protection of a pack...well, there's nothing much safer."

"I can't stay here with him."

"Why?"

"Because!"

"He has done nothing but help you. He saved both our lives this morning, Nessie. He obviously wants to protect you."

"He is not my father!"

Charlie pressed his lips together. Now he knew why the Alpha had offered them protection so easily. And why he would continue to offer the pack's protection. Nessie, as his daughter, couldn't be refused without challenging the Alpha directly. "Accepting his protection doesn't mean you have to have a relationship with him."

Nessie looked up at him. "She never loved my dad. She married him for the protection. She was in love with...with..."

"Talon," he finished for her. Nessie flinched and nodded.

He reached out for her, but she stepped away, scowling at him, and he sighed. "We can't choose who we love, Ness. Look at me. Falling for a stubborn human slave that turned out to be something else entirely wasn't exactly part of my master plan." Hell, it wasn't part of any plan. Period.

Nessie's eyes widened and he knew she had caught his meaning. And from the doe-eyed look she was giving him, she was about to make a run for it again.

"I'm not expecting you to feel the same, or even be ready to think about love." He looked away, trying to prepare himself for the inevitable rejection he was about to receive. "I understand why you're holding back. I deserve it, really."

Nessie's wide eyes gazed up at him as silence stretched between them. "You terrify me," she muttered as she continued to hold him captive. "You're the most dangerous person in my life."

He shook his head, dumbfounded. How could she even think that?

"I don't want to love you," she croaked, emotions dripping into her soft voice. "I want to hate you. For leaving me. For turning me. For...for making me feel things I don't want to. I'm overwhelmed and confused, and I don't like it!"

His heart was pounding, the echo of it loud in his ears, but he caught every word she said. Her words resonated with him on a deep level. "I felt the same way. When I got back to the mansion, the last thing I wanted was to fall in love. I had a plan, and you weren't part of it. But as soon as I tasted you, I recognized you for what you really were. My mate. And I wasn't exactly thrilled about it."

Nessie held up a hand. "Whoa, whoa, whoa. Mate?"

Yeah, he'd just opened that giant can of worms, hadn't he?

Nessie kept her gaze locked on Charlie as he cleared his throat, shuffling his feet as he stared at the ground. "Well," he started. "Each vampire has a single mate destined to share eternity with. It is through blood that mates are recognized, claimed, and bound together."

Nessie quirked her brow at him. "And you think I'm yours?"

He glared down at her in response. "I don't 'think,' I know. I knew it the moment I first tasted you back at the mansion. Once a mate is recognized, it is nearly impossible to ignore the connection."

She stood there, dumbfounded at the sheer insanity of it all. Because it sounded batshit crazy. But some small part of her realized that ever since Charlie had returned, she felt...drawn to him. His voice. His face. Even his fangs made her knees want to wobble. And it wasn't because she found fangs sexy on just anyone. Only him. But was that just remnants of her childhood crush resurfacing? Or was there something more to this?

He rolled his eyes once he saw her expression, huffing in exasperation. "Look, I don't expect you to believe it. I'm confident that in time you'll recognize me for what I am."

"And that is?"

The look in his eyes became so intense, she could feel herself falling into his gaze. "Your soulmate."

He took her hand, and she was too captivated by him to snatch it away like she should. He closed his eyes and lifted her hand up to place a tender kiss on the inside of her wrist. Heat bloomed at that one small gesture of affection. She felt her body react in an instant as his eyes opened, still vibrant blue as he pressed his lips against her skin a second time. Her stomach fluttered as he watched her face.

He smirked at her. "Your eyes are turning black," he whispered. As he said the words, she watched as his eyes darkened, the black slowly swallowing his pupil.

"So are yours."

CHAPTER TWENTY THREE

H E LOWERED HIS FACE, HIS GAZE LOCKED ON HER mouth. "So they are."

Her heart raced. She should back away. Kissing him was dangerous. She pulled her hand out of his, stepping back even though she wanted to fall right into him.

You can't run from this. Deep down, you know how you really feel. Even if you won't say it out loud.

She bit her lip as she heard his voice. That sweet, sexy voice speaking to her in the most intimate way. This couldn't happen. She couldn't love the person who broke her heart and then made it stop beating.

His jaw clenched. *I'm also the person...who made it start*

beating again. His black eyes bore into her as he laid his palm on her chest. *Listen. Close your eyes and listen.*

She swallowed the giant lump that lodged in her throat. But as she let the sounds of the forest fade into the background, she heard it. Two hearts, thrumming to the same exact beat.

Gasping, her eyes popped open, finding his still focused on her face. "How?" Vampires were...dead. How in the hell were their hearts beating?

His lips curved, drawing her attention to them and making that heartbeat of hers pick up its pace. He ran his fingers through her hair, stepping closer. The heat from his body and the smell of him making her brain fuzzy. *Our hearts lie dormant and unmoving until our mate comes along, and we are awakened. If you hadn't found your mate, you would feel cold and numb all the time.* His fingers slid down her neck, a gentle touch that set fire to her body. *Tell me, Nessie. Do you feel cold right now?*

She hadn't realized that she'd leaned her head to the side, seeking more of his magic touch. Because it made her feel like he'd lit a match on her skin. His fingers brushed down her chest to grasp her hips, his eyes blazing with unquenched desire.

And you can hear my voice tickling the inside of your mind.

Nodding, she let her head fall back as she gazed up at him, entranced. Even inside her mind, his voice lowered, husky and sexy as hell. Matching the look in his dark gaze.

Yes, she thought. *And even in my head, you talk too much.*

Charlie smiled down at her, a sly curve of his luscious-looking lips. *Do you want me to stop talking, then?*

She couldn't stop herself from nodding, and that tiny tilt of her head was all he needed. His hands gripped her hips a little tighter as he leaned down. She raised up on her toes, meeting him halfway as he claimed her mouth. Everything else fell away until there was only him - his scent enveloping her, his touch emblazing her, his heart beating in her ears.

His heart. Beating. For her. As his fingers slid up her chest, grazing her nipples into hard peaks, all thoughts ceased. She wanted him, hot and hard and breathless, and she was done denying it. She needed to satiate this relentless desire for him once and for all.

Nails lengthening, she slit the front of his shirt, pulling it from his body in one swift yank. She didn't give him time to react as a soft snap preceded his leather belt flying through the air after his shirt. His jeans followed soon after, falling to a heap on the ground.

She broke the kiss, stepping back from him, her gaze greedy for his bare skin. And wouldn't you know it. He'd gone commando. Sweetness. Practically panting for him already, he was oh-so-cooperative as he allowed her a long leisurely gawk. The size of the smirk on his face told her he knew she liked what she saw. Well, duh. Anyone with a hankering for man-candy would.

She stepped forward ready to devour him, but he held a stiff arm out, blocking her advance.

His smirk widened. "My turn," he said, his eyes twinkling at her.

He pulled her closer, turning her to face away from him. Sweeping the long length of her hair off her shoulder to bare her skin, he trailed whispers of a kiss over her sensitive flesh. Liquid heat pooled low in her belly already craving the fangs she once despised so strongly.

He continued his soft assault on her skin, however, without a hint of fang. His hands slid down her torso, his fingers grasping the hem of her shirt. He peeled it off her inch by inch, the back of his fingers grazing along her navel and over her breasts. She sucked in a breath as cold air swept over her bared flesh. Tugging it over her head, he let it join his scattered clothes on the ground. The warmth of his hands as they stroked her arm, gliding down to press circles into the inside of her wrist, had her sighing and leaning back against his body.

One of those deliciously warm hands cupped her breast, his thumb toying with the nipple and drawing a soft gasp from her. She arched back, pushing her chest into his hand in a silent request for more. His free hand tipped her chin, turning her face as he captured her lips in a scorching kiss. She could feel the hard length of him push against her backside as he tasted her mouth, swiping his tongue over her fangs, sending sparks of pleasure through her body, straight to her core.

Sweet gods! Fangs were definitely erogenous. She moaned into his mouth, grinding her ass against him. He nipped at her lip and plucked her nipple roughly before turning his attention to her other breast. The combination of pleasure and pain had her knees weakening, her supernatural strength useless against his magic touch.

He teased her into a frenzy, relentless in his assault on her, his hands everywhere. Everywhere except where she wanted them most.

"Please," she begged, her voice breathless.

He nipped at her shoulder, teasing her with his fangs. Those damn fangs he refused to bite her with! "Please what?" he whispered against her skin. "What do you want, Nessie?"

Her fingers flew up, sinking into his short strands of dark hair and pulling...hard. She arched into his body, pushing back against his erection. "Touch me," she demanded.

She heard him growl low in his throat, a primal, animalistic sound that vibrated through her, awakening all her feminine instincts. A moment later, his hand slid down her body, pushing under the waistband of her jeans.

She cried out as his fingers found her sweet spot. Good gods, finally! He stroked her until she was breathless. When the jeans proved restricting to his access, he growled before easily tearing them open and delving lower, pushing a finger into her core. Her knees gave out as pleasure robbed her of balance. He caught her with his spare arm, wrapping it around her torso and pulling her back to lean against the strength of his body as he pumped his finger, his thumb rotating the tiny nub that sent her head reeling.

"Come for me," he whispered against her skin, his voice husky.

When he added another finger and swirled them inside her, she fell over the edge, spiraling as the waves of pleasure crashed over her. When only the aftershocks remained, he slid his hand out of her jeans, pulling them down her legs as she regained her balance.

When she was devoid of all clothing, he stepped around her, surveying her from arm's length. She stepped to close the distance, but he shook his finger. "Now, fair is fair. I let you have your turn," he teased.

"You've got to be kidding me. Well, you took your sweet ass time taking your turn."

He smiled. "You bet your sweet ass I did." His fingers gripped said sweet ass, pulling her toward him. "And I enjoyed every sweet ass moment of it."

She rolled her eyes not able to stop her lips from curving into a smile. He leaned down, capturing her smiling lips with his mouth. At some point, her hands roved over his body, scorching a trail down his abdomen. When she took him in her hand, his breath hitched. She slid her fingers over him, amazed by the soft firmness of it. Like velvet steel. He closed his eyes, his mouth opening in a silent moan. Exhilaration streaked through her as she continued to explore him, watching the pleasure wash over his features. Her body bloomed with heat as she coaxed each sound of pleasure from his delectable mouth.

A curse flew from his lips a moment before he pulled himself from her grasp, hauling her up against a tree. He fell to his knees.

"I'm going to put my mouth on you now," he said. It was not a request, not a question. No, it was a warning. And he didn't wait for a response.

His hands pushed her thighs apart just before he took her in his mouth. *Oh, my sweet heavens.* She cried out, reaching her hands up to grab the trunk of the tree for support, not trusting her weak knees where this man was concerned. He made love to her with his mouth, his fangs teasing her in the most erotic way. She heard his moan join hers, the vibrations of his mouth throwing her body over the edge, making her scream his name.

He growled against her as he continued to pleasure her with his mouth, not allowing her to recover before her body was building toward another release.

Her fingers gripped his hair, pulling until he finally lifted his head and gazed up at her.

"If you make me do that again without you inside me, I swear I will cut off your head."

He smirked and pulled her down to him, dropping sweet kisses over her as he laid her amongst the pile of clothes. His hands landed on the crook of her elbows, sliding them up over her head where he held her in place. Looking down at her, he paused as the tip of him nudged against her. Her back arched off the ground as another streak of pleasure tore through her.

"Are you sure?" he asked.

She pulled her legs up, groaning as the movement had her core sliding over the head of him.

His grip tightened on her arms as his eyes sparkled like black diamonds. "Dammit, Nessie. You are testing my control."

She wriggled beneath him, desperate to get him inside her. "Good, that was my goal."

He groaned, closing his eyes as he bent his head down and kissed her senseless. Her hips began bucking on their own, desperate for him, feeling empty. His lips trailed kisses down her jaw, and she turned her head to the side.

He moved against her core as his mouth pressed against her throat, his hot tongue making her skin tingle.

She felt a tiny sting as his fangs pierced her skin, and then white-hot streaks of pleasure zinged through her. His grip tightened, holding her body still as he pushed inside her. As he suckled at her throat, each pull sending another streak of pleasure through her, she barely noticed the slight discomfort of his invasion, pressing into her an inch at a time.

He was torturing himself. The heat of her body wrapped around him like a perfectly fitted glove, and his languid pace was nearly impossible to continue. The urge to bury himself inside her hard and fast had nearly overwhelmed him as her intoxicating blood filled his mouth.

Don't hurt her again. The thought kept his more animal instincts in check. Finally, after several long minutes, he was buried to the hilt. He took one last pull from her throat before releasing his fangs and sealing the wound shut with a slow glide of his tongue.

He forced himself to remain still, allowing her to adjust to him, watching as the blissful haze his bite had caused subsided. He waited for any signs of pain to cross her face, and when only lust and a hint of impatience stared back at him, he began to test her readiness. Slowly, he moved, pulling his hips back slightly, their eyes locked as he pushed himself deep inside her again. With the fog his bite had put her in lifted, she was feeling him move inside her for the first time. And her face lit up beautifully.

Her mouth opened in a silent gasp, as if surprised by the sensation. Still, no pain. He repeated the motion, gyrating his hips slowly. True, untainted pleasure spread across her face. Her arms moved beneath his grasp. Was it too much for her? Had he gone too fast? Bracing himself for her rejection, he released his hold on her and started to retreat from the warmth of her body.

She stopped his retreat quickly, her legs pulling up, wringing a groan from him as she wrapped them around his waist, pulling him deep within. Her cry of pleasure joined his as he felt her hands slide down his back. He watched her eyes close as he thrust inside her, the delicious friction of their movements sending shockwaves through him.

"More," Nessie demanded with a moan.

The last thread of his control snapped like a pitiful twig.

"Ah, gods," he moaned as he pumped into her, her hips meeting his every thrust.

He reared up, lifting her as he sat back on his ankles. She unwound her legs from his waist as her hands pulled his face toward hers for a blistering kiss that demanded his complete surrender. A moment later, she began moving over him, taking control from him in one swift maneuver as her body rode his. She left a scorching trail of kisses down his throat, and a moment later, her fangs sank into the meat of his shoulder.

Cocooning her in his arms, he felt his body begin to lose all control, pleasure building and concentrating. He felt the pull as she drew more blood from his body, and he couldn't stop himself. The need to mark his mate was too great to ignore. He buried his fangs within her flesh a second time as he thrust his hips up, slamming into her. All restraint lost to this one perfect moment.

She tore her fangs from him on a scream as she arched her back and cried to the heavens. Her nails bit into his back as he clutched her tighter, slipping his fangs from her creamy flesh as his own cry of release joined hers, a rush of pride filling his chest as he saw the tiny fang marks permanently scarred into her chest.

They collapsed to the ground, her body rolling to the side, her limbs sprawled over his body. Gasping to catch her breath, she gazed up at the sky, still amazed by how clearly she could see the canopy of the forest around her and the stars peeking through the leaves. She had to admit that the night vision was an awesome perk.

Charlie stirred beside her, his arms wrapping around her body and pulling her against his chest, resting his cheek against her forehead. "You're amazingly good at this. Are you sure this was your first time?"

He chuckled and she swiftly elbowed him in the ribs, making him grunt. Of course, it was. And, she had to admit it had been an amazing start.

Start? This was a one and done deal, remember? she reminded herself.

"One and done? What the fuck does that mean?" Charlie raised up on his elbows, looking down at her, his eyebrows pinched together.

"Ummm..." For once, she couldn't come up with any response. It was supposed to be over now. She'd gotten what she'd needed.

Shock and disgust blanketed his face as he pushed her off him. "Are you fucking kidding me?" He got to his feet, slamming his legs into his jeans. "So, all you wanted was my dick?"

Jumping to her feet, she threw her hands in the air. "What did you expect me to do? Swoon like a pathetic teenager? Actually buy into your 'mate' talk bullshit."

The words even stung her as she bit them out.

He shook his head, throwing his shirt back over his head. "You're a fucking piece of work," he mumbled, turning his eyes away.

But she saw them. Tears pooling in those beautiful blue eyes and seeing them made her chest ache. She buried it because she didn't know how to be a mate. Hell, did she even want to be one?

"Well, this 'piece of work' needs more than five minutes to jump into eternity with the guy that broke my fucking heart," she snapped, grabbing her clothes and throwing them on.

"Yeah. Go ahead, Ness. Run away," he mumbled.

She narrowed her gaze on him. "I learned from the best, didn't I?" She stomped away, her chest clenching. Because she'd hurt him. On purpose. But this time, she'd instantly regretted it.

Charlie stared after Nessie as she ran away from him so fast she was barely even a blur. What the fuck just happened?

He punched the tree beside him, making it crack and causing sap to leak all over his hand. He cursed, trying to get the tears to dry up.

How had he ended up in this mess? He'd never wanted a mate in the first place. And now, now she was the only thing he wanted. And he couldn't get her to let her walls down. Those walls he'd built with each day he'd been absent. It would seem they'd take just as long to come down.

Well, it's a good thing I'm immortal, isn't it? Because patience was one thing he excelled at.

Charlie's head jerked as he heard rustling close by. His mind had been so wrapped up in his fucking mate that he hadn't noticed a group of lycans trailing right towards him. He turned, ready to take off after Nessie. But no. That would lead this group right to her. So, he took off in another direction, but he hadn't even made a few hundred yards when a familiar scent wafted towards him. A certain lycan he'd drained a few pints of blood from.

"Don't tell me that feisty human bitch wore you out, bloodsucker," the beast who'd tried to violate Nessie stood larger than life before him, sneering down his long nose. His smug of evil matched his dark, beady eyes perfectly. "Go ahead and yell. I'd love to get her back in my hands when she comes to find you."

Charlie clenched his jaw and tried to leap at him. Unfortunately, two more mutts came from behind and clutched each arm, holding him in place. The big bad wolf was smarter than he looked. Charlie could have overpowered him in human form easily. Too bad.

The ugly brute leaned closer, getting in his face. "I'm waiting."

Charlie spat at him. "Fuck you, beast."

He'd expected an outburst of rage. Lycans were known for their short fuses. But this one was all calm and collected as he wiped his mug, not looking the least bit upset. If anything, he looked amused.

"Beast," he said, nodding. "I like that." He looked into Charlie's eyes and smiled before gripping Charlie's jaw and pulling him close. "And that beauty of yours is *mine*."

The fuck she is! Charlie's fangs snapped at him, making the monster jerk his head back.

Crack! A swift backhand to the cheek jerked Charlie's head to the side, making him see spots.

Damn, the man had some strength despite being in human form. He would not want to fuck with this one in wolf form. No, thank you.

The beast kicked him, boot smashing into his face and making his head fly back. Fuuuuck. He was never gonna sleep in these woods again. The two smaller lycans continued to hold him up as the beast pummeled him a few more times.

"C'mon. Yell for help. I want that pretty little human to watch her precious bloodsucker die before I take her."

Charlie glared at him. Fuck that shit. He'd die before he let this maniac anywhere near Nessie.

The beast went to hit him again, but another lycan, hairy as a wooly mammoth, stepped in. "Jaxon, we don't want to draw attention. We are in Whitemoon territory. They will overtake us if they come out in force."

Jaxon looked as if he might just kill the man for speaking, but a moment later, he nodded. "Fine. We take him alive, though." Jaxon threw a sneer his way. "His bitch will come looking for him."

Fucking bastard! Now, he was bait! Charlie threw the two lycans off him, catching them off guard. He went for Jaxon, ready to tear his head from his shoulders with his bare fangs and gorge on his blood. The hairy one stepped in his path, slowing his advance as he grabbed an arm and spun, hearing a loud snap as the elbow broke. The lycan roared as Charlie shoved him to the side.

His vision locked on Jaxon, who looked way too fucking calm. Before he could rip the bastard a new breathing hole, several arms grabbed him from behind. He fought to shrug them off, but there were too many.

Jaxon strode up to him, grabbed the back of his head and jaw, and jerked. The last thing he felt was his spine snap before the void took him.

CHAPTER TWENTY FOUR

NESSIE'S SKIN PRICKLED. DAWN WAS CLOSE. TOO close. Her gaze darted over the line of trees that edged the village. Where the hell was he?

She waited another minute before she headed for the tree line. Patience had never been her strong suit.

Suddenly, Torin stood in front of her. She snapped her teeth at him. "Get the hell out of my way." She tried to go around him, but he blocked her again, his arms crossing over his chest as he jerked his chin to the left.

Talon walked towards her, Eva at his side. Nessie's fists clenched.

"Where do you think you're going this close to dawn?" Talon

asked, his voice curt. He was obviously used to getting what he asked. Well, shit on that.

"None of your goddamn business," she snapped, lifting her chin.

Talon's gaze, way too similar to her own, narrowed.

Torin got in her face. "Don't speak to him like that, you filthy bloodsucker!"

Nessie shoved him away, sending him flying into a pile of baskets a few yards away.

"It's Charlie," Eva said softly, her eyes on Nessie.

Nessie frowned at her. "He's not back yet. I'm going to find him."

"Don't be stupid. Dawn is near," Talon said.

"I won't leave him out there to burn!"

Talon shook his head. "I will send out a search party. And you will get inside." He nodded toward Torin, who gave Nessie a nasty look, but went to gather the search party.

"Stop telling me what to do." Nessie glared at Talon and her mother as they stood side by side. "I don't care who you fucked, he is not my father, and he never will be."

Nessie's skin burned with frustration. Her father was dead, her sperm donor was a hairy monster by moonlight, and where the hell was Charlie?! She eyed the line of trees.

"Don't even think about it," Talon snapped. "The search party will find him. Plus, he's got more experience getting out of the sun than you do."

Nessie recalled asking Charlie about getting out of the sun in a pinch. "Underground," she muttered. She looked up at Talon. "Charlie said if necessary, we could bury ourselves to escape the sun."

Talon nodded. "I'll let the search party know to look for any loose piles of earth, but they won't be able to uncover him until after the sun goes down."

Eva rubbed her arm. "They'll find him, dear. Lycans are some of the best trackers in the world."

Nessie wanted to shrug her mother's hand off her. She was still pissed at her for keeping so many secrets. The truth of her heritage for one thing. But the deep-seated concern written on the woman's face made her hesitate. "I should be helping them," she told her.

Eva smiled at her. "I know you feel that way, but you know that's not possible. I'm afraid you're going to have to sit out on the action this time." Her fingers closed around Nessie's hand, her smile unwavering. She jerked her head toward the house to the right - Talon's. Groan. "C'mon. Let's get you inside where it's safe."

Nessie wrinkled her nose at her. Eva just chuckled at her, rolled her eyes, and tugged her hand, pulling her toward the house. Nessie slumped her shoulders and followed her mother.

Once in the safety of the large basement, she began pacing. Visions of a crispy Charlie replayed in her mind whenever she tried to lie down, so she asked Eva to get her something to do. Unfortunately, there wasn't much to choose from. The primitive village was a far cry from the cultural hubs and history-rich cities the vampires occupied. No hologram televisions, no museums, theaters, or shops. At least in the mansion she had a library of books to keep her mind occupied. Here it was nothing but four walls, a bed, and a closet full of linens and cleaning supplies. What the hell did these lycans do in their spare time?

Eva chuckled and Nessie looked back at her, finding her mother looking highly amused. "What?" she asked.

Her mother replied, "Lycans are a very primitive species. Unlike vampires, they don't come from a human background and have a much stronger connection to nature than they do to human history or culture. That's why you don't see any of the frivolities and luxuries that Jack's mansion possessed."

Nessie hadn't realized she'd voiced her question out loud. Although, her mother still hadn't quite answered her question. "So, what do they do in their spare time, then?"

Eva's sly smile had her second guessing wanting the answer. Her mother gave it to her anyway. "Lycans are very in tune with their physical needs. They spend most of their time tending to them."

Nessie raised an eyebrow. "Physical needs?" Gods, did she really want to know?

"Sleep, sustenance, and sex."

Nessie rolled her eyes. She'd suspected as much, especially since she'd jumped Charlie's bones a few hours ago. "I'm surprised there aren't more little furry monsters running around then."

Eva's smile faded. "There are. Male ones, at least. Offspring are few and far between, but lycans are immortal like vampires. Me and Talon were blessed when we conceived you. A mixed couple has never conceived a female of their kind." Eva took her hand in her own, guiding them to sit on the edge of the bed. "You have always been a special girl, Nessie. My little miracle. But you need to heed my advice in this. We must stay with Talon's pack. I know you don't want to," she continued as Nessie opened her mouth to argue. "But you are in a great deal of danger still. These woods are filled with lycan packs. For hundreds of miles. Nothing but wilderness and wolves. Trust me. You are the most valued commodity in their world, Nessie. They will do anything...anything...to get you."

Nessie studied her mother. The hard set of her jaw, wide-set eyes focused solely on her, and her hands clutching her own. The woman meant every word. Nessie's head tilted to the side. "Why would they value me? I was just a slave. And now, I'm a...I don't even know what I am."

"They never saw you for what you were. You had never transformed fully. Your scent was human like mine. Outwardly, you appeared completely human. But you're not."

Nessie took a deep breath as her mother reminded her of her unavoidable link to Talon and the pack. "I know. But why does that matter? You said so yourself, there are tons of them running in these parts."

Eva shook her head. "Not females. That is what makes you so valuable. Female lycans are extremely rare, an entire pack can go centuries before one is born. Ninety-nine percent of their population is male."

Nessie shrugged. "I still don't get the big deal. There are plenty of human women like you to take care of those 'needs'."

Eva smirked. "While that is true, only lycanas can birth their own kind. Well, until you. And unlike human women, all of their offspring are lycans no matter what the father is. It's why Talon's father was so against us marrying. There had been a female lycan born in the pack, and his father had arranged for Talon to marry her instead when she came of age."

Nessie felt the urge to hug her mother as the memory had clearly saddened her. "So, Talon's wife is a lycana?"

Eva shook her head. "No. No, she's human as well."

Nessie's brows clenched. "Then what the hell was the point of denying your marriage?"

"The female lycan didn't live past her second birthday. Lycanas are very fragile in infancy. It happened after I had already been captured. At that point, there were only human females left to choose from."

Nessie studied her mother a moment. She was obviously crushed at losing Talon, which made her think of Charlie. And while she hated to admit it, she, too, would be crushed if she lost him, which was a very real possibility. Just the thought chilled her blood and made her want to crawl into a deep ditch and wither away.

Her mother grabbed her hand. "You are especially unique, Nessie. A true blend of the supernatural species. Every pack will want to get their hands on you. You could potentially be the only vampire able to produce children."

"Then why should I stay with *this* pack?"

Sighing, her mother stroked her cheek. "Because it's my pack. I was born here. Raised here. This was my family. Is my family. And now, it's your family, too. I'm not asking you to forget your father." Nessie tensed as she mentioned the man who raised her, and his unfortunate demise. "I'm just asking you to give your new one a chance. Let them protect us. Please. I don't want to lose you again."

They both jumped as the front door upstairs crashed open and several heavy footsteps padded across the ceiling. The basement door clicked open and soon the room filled with a handful of males, including Talon, Torin, and several others she had yet to meet.

Torin stood next to his father, arms crossed and scowling. He obviously hadn't gotten over their little scuff earlier. Like she cared.

When none of the brooding males spoke up, Nessie huffed. "Well? Did you find him or not?" *Please don't say he's dead. Please don't say he's dead.*

Talon exchanged looks with Torin, who shrugged his shoulders nonchalantly. Talon faced her. "We were able to track him," he stated.

A few seconds ticked by as Nessie's heart raced like a freight train. When Talon didn't continue, she had the urge to smack the words out of him. "And? Where is he?" Why the hell was everyone being so hesitant? Just spit it out!

"Blackmoon's got him," Torin said, his scowl deepening if that was even possible.

"Blackmoon?" she asked. What the hell was that?

"It's a neighboring pack. With an Alpha the size of a black bear."

Nessie's heart stopped. Literally. Bam. Racing one moment...dead still the next. Not a peep from the soppy son of a bitch that did cartwheels whenever Charlie was around. That giant black monster of a wolf had Charlie in his claws. And after Charlie had nearly ripped his head off, she doubted he'd be too friendly to his new captive. Her eyes searched Talon's face. "Is he...is he..." Gods, she couldn't even say it!

"No, he's not dead. We would have smelled the ash. For some reason, he's keeping him alive."

She exhaled a long breath she hadn't realized she'd held in. She clenched her fist, growling under her breath, "I know why."

Talon and Torin quirked their brows, their expressions identical. "Why?"

It was Nessie's turn to scowl. "Bait."

The males muttered among themselves. Most of them wondering why Blackmoon would care about a bloodsucker.

"Charlie interrupted him 'claiming' his new slave," Nessie started. "And now he thinks Charlie will lure me back so he can finish the job."

"You?" Torin asked, snickering. "Why the hell would an Alpha care about claiming a bloodsucker, like you?"

Nessie's fists clenched as she took a step toward the arrogant prick. Talon held up a hand and turned toward his son. "She is not a bloodsucker."

Torin rolled his eyes. "She snapped those fangs at me more than once." His eyes narrowed to slits as he watched her. She was about to give the little prick an up-close and personal look at her fangs if he kept calling her a bloodsucker. Said prick's eyes widened suddenly as his gaze met hers.

"As you can see, son, her eyes glow gold like ours." Talon had turned toward the small group of males that stood huddled around the stairs. Each masculine face turned toward her, expressions ranging from shock and confusion to anger and disbelief.

"What is this bullshit?" a scruffy blonde male asked as his pale green eyes narrowed on her.

Torin remained silent as his gaze, gold beginning to creep into his hazel irises, darted over her face.

Talon stepped forward and turned toward the scrutinizing males. With his body situated slightly in front of her, Nessie had to lean to the side to see Torin's face. His eyes were locked on his father's now as his head began shaking.

"Yes, my son. What you suspect is true." Talon's voice softened as he continued. "She is my daughter."

There was a mixture of gasps and curses among the group, but Torin remained speechless, only his head shaking as his lip curled and his jaw twitched.

"Which makes her your sister," Talon said.

There was a sharp intake of breath, and it took Nessie a moment to realize it had been her. Torin was her brother. Somehow, she hadn't thought of that before now.

"No," Torin snapped. "No, you're lying." Torin squeezed his eyes shut and turned away from them.

Talon took a step forward and put his hand on his son's shoulder. Talon went on to tell how Nessie came to be, and what had happened to Eva that had torn the two away from the pack. Slowly, Torin's fists unclenched. His gaze met hers, no longer narrowed in suspicion, but open in genuine curiosity. A brother seeing his sister for the first time.

"You didn't know either, did you?" he asked.

Nessie shook her head. "No, not at first. I overheard my mother talking to Talon. That's how I found out." She took a tentative step forward, the corner of her mouth curving upward. "And, compared to me, you handled the news pretty well, actually. I guess we know who the hothead in the family is."

Torin managed a weak smile in return before looking toward his father. Following his gaze, Nessie found Talon smiling at the two of them. His hazel eyes, the exact shade of his children's, sparkled with pride. Nessie gulped at the familiar look, one her father - the one who raised her - gave her frequently. Apparently, even a monster could feel the bonds of love and family. She realized as she gazed around at the new faces in her life that they had already accepted her. She was one of them. Lycan. Vampire. Human. All of the above. It didn't matter. She was family. And they had her back. Just like Charlie had her back ever since coming back. It was time she return the favor.

Clearing her throat, she took a breath. Enough of the touchy feely. Time to get down to business. "At dusk, I'm going for Charlie."

Talon turned on her. "What? That's madness! You can't take on an entire pack by yourself!"

Sticking her chin in the air, she said, "I guess we'll see, won't we?" Talon's gaze bore into her, and she stared right back.

Finally, after several minutes of silence, Talon closed his eyes and sighed. "You're as stubborn as your mother."

"Don't even try to stick that on me," her mother teased.

Nessie stuck her tongue out at him, not caring if he saw. Which he did and rolled his eyes, smiling. "Given that he is your chosen mate-"

Nessie took a step back. "Whoa, whoa. I didn't say anything about -"

"Oh, please, Vanessa," her mother said. "If you're willing to take on an entire wolf pack to save him, then you've claimed him. And by the looks of that mark on your chest. He's claimed you as well."

Nessie looked down at her chest, heat rising in her cheeks as sure enough, there it was. Charlie's fang marks scarred into her chest. She tried to think back. Had she left the same marks on him back in the woods?

The thought of calling Charlie "mate" terrified the ever-living shit out of her. It also had her heart doing flippin' acrobatics.

"Are you willing to leave him to his fate at Blackmoon?" Talon asked.

If Jaxon was half the dickhead she thought him to be...

Raising her chin, she met Talon's gaze unblinking. "Hell no." *He's mine.*

Talon nodded. "Very well. As your chosen mate, Charlie is entitled to the protection of the pack as well."

Several more curses flew through the room.

"The fuck he is!"

"He's a bloodsucker!"

"What is this shit?"

Talon spun. "Shut the fuck up, all of you!"

Cricket. Cricket.

Well, damn, the man had skills.

CHAPTER TWENTY FIVE

"WHY ISN'T HE DEAD YET?"

"Jaxon wants him alive. I think he has a hard-on for that human that got away a few days ago, and he thinks this bloodsucker is her lover."

A grunt of approval. "Bloodsucker bait. I like it."

Charlie didn't bother opening his eyes. He already knew at least two mongrels stood guard. Plus, he had the migraine of a fucking demon right now. Coming back from the dead...again...didn't come without its side effects. The rest of his body screamed in silent agony, so, yeah, he was content with lying still at the moment. Motherfucking mutts must have had a field day with his body before it regained a pulse.

"Yeah, but she's a stupid bitch if she comes for him. Jaxon will eat her alive."

One of them snickered. The douchebag one. "Yeah, literally. Bitch won't know what hit her."

His immortal ass needed to get its shit together and heal. Faster. Because these dickheads needed to die. Yesterday.

He heard the creak of a door and heavy footsteps. "How is my favorite prisoner?" Jaxon's unnaturally low voice clawed at Charlie's brain, making him want to wince. *Not yet. Play dead until your strength returns.* "Hasn't he reanimated yet?" A long silence ensued, then Jaxon clicked his tongue. "His heart beats, you idiots. Learn to use your fucking senses!"

Slam! Charlie groaned as the son of a bitch buried his boot in his gut. Curling his body and wrapping his arms around his midsection, he finally peeled his lids open. Jaxon smiled down at him, happy as a harpy. "Up and at 'em, sunshine," he practically sang.

Fuck. This was gonna be a long night.

Jaxon grabbed the scruff of his neck and hauled him to his feet, wobbly as they were. Smiling even wider, Jaxon released him and looked over at his companions, snickering. "You know, I've missed this. Bloodsuckers come through the area so rarely anymore that I never get to have any fun." He looked down at Charlie again, grinning like a fucking lunatic. "I want to thank you for that, my friend."

Crack! The meaty fist of the monstrous beast struck the side Charlie's face, and he felt his jaw shatter. Charlie stumbled, but managed to regain his balance.

"If he keeps going like this, he's gonna end up killing the delicate flower anyway," one of the guard dogs muttered to his companion.

Jaxon's happy face fell as he looked over at the duo. The loudmouth one snapped his mouth shut, his eyes widening as he fell silent. Jaxon took the one giant step he required to cross the tiny room, the smaller male backing into the wall at his approach. One quick jab to the face later, the mouthy one's head slammed into the wall. He crumpled to the floor, clutching his nose as it gushed blood.

A smile back on his ugly mug, Jaxon recrossed the room and threw a heavy arm over Charlie's shoulder. "Now, is that any way to talk to our new friend here, Lucus?"

Lucus' eyes widened and he shook his head rapidly.

Apparently, Lucus was the smart one of the pair. Or the cowardly one.

The door suddenly flew open as the hairy one stepped over the threshold. "Whitemoon's attacking."

Jaxon's chipper mood vanished. "Whitemoon? What the hell are they thinking? We've been at peace with them since Lauren was traded to them years ago."

The male shrugged. "It doesn't seem like they're in a peaceful discussion mood."

Jaxon removed his arm from around Charlie and began walking toward the door. "It must have been our breach of their territory lines earlier. I didn't see any of their members when we took the bloodsucker, though."

There were some masculine yells in the distance. Jaxon whipped his head around toward Lucus. "What the fuck are you waiting for? Get your ass out there!" His gaze dropped to the other one still clutching his nose on the floor. "And take his ass with you."

A moment later, Lucus hauled the other male to his feet and they both ran out the door. Jaxon turned toward him. "Unfortunately, I've got some business to take care of before we can have any fun, my friend." He slapped Charlie's shoulder, smiling. "Don't worry, I'll be back soon."

Talon and Torin had gone over some basic shifting principles with her. Her mother had explained to them that she'd only shifted when a loved one was in mortal danger and during the one hunger rage. Apparently, she could shift at will anytime the moon was out.

"You can't shift during new moons at all. And on full moons, you won't have any choice. You'll have to shift," Talon explained as the others gathered their weapons. "Well, at least that's how it is for normal lycans. We'll have to wait and see if that holds true for you."

Nessie bounced on the balls of her feet at the bottom of the basement steps. *C'mon, c'mon.* She urged the sun to move faster. She didn't have the time or patience to wait for its slow ass to drop behind the mountains. *Gods, I hate this*, she thought.

The other pack members had gone ahead of her, able to begin the attack in daylight. Lucky bastards. She understood the advantages of drawing Blackmoon's attention.

Her eyes drilled a hole into the door at the top of the stairs. Almost there. Another few moments and she'd be able to sneak her way into Blackmoon and find Charlie while the others kept Blackmoon's members busy.

Three, two, one. Nessie burst through the door, hearing the metal door groan under the force. The cold dusk air rushed over her skin as the scenery blew by in a blur.

As the familiar musk of sweaty males and dog filled the air, she slowed to a solid sprint by human standards. Circling the edge of the village, she saw the faint glow of dozens of torches that perched outside each house. When the chorus of battle faded somewhat, she crept toward the first building, slithering along the edge in silence.

Glancing up, she saw the moon crest over the canopy. She inhaled, closing her eyes as dozens of scents bombarded her. Damn it all to hell. Why did she have to be so bad at this? She couldn't pick Charlie's scent out of all the unfamiliar ones. Her eyes darted from this house to that, trying to jog her memory. Nothing. The houses all looked the same, ranging in size from a shed to a several room home.

Daring to tiptoe further toward the center, she decided the smaller buildings were the better option. The first two she came across held nothing but tools and lumber. The next one made her stomach churn with several bloody chains, daggers, whips, and devices she didn't even want to attempt to name. Had any of those been used on Charlie? She shuddered at the thought.

"I was wondering when you'd show up."

Oh shit, here we go. Nessie froze, feeling her body tense at the deep voice. She turned her head, seeing Jaxon's crooked grin widen as their eyes met.

"You humans are so predictable," he sneered, taking a step toward her.

Still thought she was human? Wonderful. At least she hadn't completely lost the element of surprise.

She smiled back sweetly, catching his gaze flicker in confusion. "Have you really been waiting around for me?" Pressing her hand to her chest, she batted her lashes at him. "I'd be flattered if you weren't such a gigantic prick."

Licking his lips, he allowed his eyes to venture over her body. "I think I'm going to like having you around. Aren't you cold in so little clothes?"

Shit. She'd forgotten. With cold no longer being such an adversary, the layers of clothes hadn't crossed her mind. Of course, she hadn't been concerned with portraying herself as human when she had left the basement in such a hurry either. She hoped the fact that she wore little more than a tank, jeans, and boots didn't alert him to her little secret.

She kept her sweet smile planted as she shrugged. "Must be the adrenaline."

His smirk widened and he rolled his shoulders. "I'm just getting your blood pumping, baby cakes."

He started striding toward her, his shoulders swaggering with every step. Arrogant scum. She felt her blood rushing in her ears, her gaze falling on the large vein pulsing at his neck. Shit!

She spun away from him, resisting the urge to run. Her gums throbbed and pain laced through her fingers. *Not yet*, she told herself. *I need him closer first.*

Her skin coiled as Jaxon ran his meaty hand up her spine. As his fingers gripped the back of her neck, he murmured in her ear, "Not even running from me, eh? I almost get the feeling you want me."

"Oh, Jaxon," she whispered, hearing his heavy breathing pause. She took a deep breath, drawing his attention to her voice, and releasing the vice-grip of control she had on her body, and hoping it worked.

Her fangs punched painfully from her gums, her fingers screaming as they lengthened and contorted, claws ripping through her fingertips. "You have no idea how badly I want you." She smiled, her pearly whites pricking along her lips. "Dead." She turned her head to look back at Jaxon, seeing her glowing gold eyes in Jaxon's pupils. Surprise, motherfucker.

Jaxon's grip loosened on her neck. "What the fuck?"

Mental high-five. Goal accomplished. Taking advantage of his state of shock, Nessie slammed an elbow into his wide-eyed mug, making him stumble back. She was on him in an instant, sinking her claws through the flesh of his chest and climbing up his large body. His carotid a beacon to her rising hunger. Allowing her new instincts to overcome her, she slammed into his throat to access the blood that made the monster tick. Let's drain this deranged dog.

He groaned, his arms clutching her against him, making her pause as she gorged on him. That was *not* a groan of pain. When she felt something solid press against her groin, she froze. Was this crazy fuck getting off? She tore her fangs from his flesh, hearing him moan as she pushed her claws deeper into his chest, trying to force his body off her.

His eyes were wide and wild. Bat shit crazy. What the hell did she just do?

"Oh, baby, I think I might have just fallen in love with you."

Oh. Hell. No. She licked the blood from her lips, watching his gaze flicker down to her mouth, his pupils dilating. Shit, this was bad. Oh, bad, bad, bad. No more fang action for this lunatic. She slammed her head up, pain bursting through her skull as it connected with his face. There was a satisfying crunch as Jaxon's head flung back, blood pouring from his now-distorted nose. She pulled her knees up in the widened space between their bodies, her feet climbing his chest and kicking him off her. He flew twenty feet in the air as she rolled to her stomach and jumped to her feet.

Her body shifted, bones bending and snapping into their new place. The form-fitting clothes she wore split at the seams to accommodate her growing figure. She turned in place as the thud of Jaxon's feet on the grass reached her ears.

Blood dripped down her chin, her eyes locking onto Jaxon's. *Ah, shit, here we go*, she thought as Jaxon's dark eyes shone gold.

"You are a beautiful creature," he murmured as if he was right next to her ear instead of thirty feet away. His voice contorted, deepening even further, until it was lost to his growing snout.

"Well, you're not," she said, swiping her clawed hand through the air. However, her own voice sounded completely foreign to her. The voice of a monster, low and growling.

Jaxon chuckled and roared as his shoulder jerked out of its socket. Nessie watched in awe as the larger-than-life man morphed into the larger-than-life wolf with fur as dark as his soul. He shook out his thick coat and stretched his limbs as they popped back into place.

His gold gaze locked with hers for a moment, and she could swear she saw his wolfish grin before he snapped his teeth and charged.

She grinned back, bending her knees. Unlike the beast before her, she was not restricted to four legs. Thanks to her vampire side she assumed, she retained the ability to walk on two legs, along with her handy opposable thumbs.

He would go for her throat as any common beast would. She spun to get out of reach, but his jaw clamped down on her ankle. Damn. He wasn't as predictable as she thought. She twisted her torso, gripped his snout with both hands and wrenched his jaw open. He growled as she pulled her foot out of his mouth.

Pushing off his giant snout, she flipped out of reach and bolted. She had always been fast by human standards, but that had been because of her lycan genes and not natural talent, unfortunately. Jaxon was nipping at her heels in no time flat. Maybe four legs were better than two. Dammit.

Masculine cries of war grew louder with every step. The others were close. Too close. Not needing Jaxon calling for his buddies to come help, she veered away from the sounds. Risking a glance back, she skipped a step to keep her calf from being devoured by Jaxon's massive mouth. A second snap of his jaws followed, making her lose her balance as she tried to jump out of reach.

She crashed to the ground, barely catching herself before her face had a much too intimate moment with the dirt. Jaxon's heavy body pressed down on hers, nearly suffocating her. Clawing at the ground, yanking hunks of grass out, she tried to slither from beneath him. Fat chance. She coughed, needing air, loose dirt flying up her nose. More coughing.

Jaxon's teeth clamped down on her shoulder. Hard. She screamed, but it came out as a roar. Oh, right. Not human. She stilled. When her brain didn't go fuzzy and shut down on her, she smiled. Apparently, oxygen was no longer a necessity. *Thank you, Charlie.*

When the pain from Jaxon's brutal bite subsided a bit, she tried to buck him off her. *You've got to be kidding me. Is he humping me like a fucking dog? Seriously!* The rhythmic movement of his hips slamming into her ass made her gag. When she couldn't simply muscle him off her, she tried to slam her head into his, but his fat wolf head was too high up.

He began wheezing. Wait. Was he laughing at her? Son of a bitch! She flailed beneath him, whimpering as his teeth sank deeper into the flesh of her shoulder, scraping along her flesh. She grit her teeth to keep from screaming. When she peeled her eyes open, Jaxon's arms morphed beside her returning to human. Talon had mentioned that lycans could shift at will under the moon.

"Can't get you properly naked without some nimble fingers," he purred into her ear. His fingers dug under the waistband of her torn jeans.

She let out a laugh, making him pause.

"You find this amusing?" he asked.

"Well, yeah. You changed back." *Giving up your advantage, dumbass.* "Just so you could take my clothes off?"

His lips curved into a smile as he pressed his mouth against her throat. "Well, I can't very well fuck you with these on," he murmured, tugging on her waistband.

She laughed harder.

"What the fuck is so funny?" He sounded irritated.

She peered back at him, seeing the shiny gold of her eyes still reflected in his dark brown ones. "You really are a big, dumb dog, aren't you?"

His mouth fell open as his eyes narrowed. "You little bi---"

Reaching up over her head, she dug her claws (because *she* wasn't a dumb fuck who changed back to a weaker form in the middle of battle) into the sides of his face, relishing in the roar she drew from him. His weight lifted as he tried to pull his face away, giving her some precious leverage. She slammed her body up, finally able to buck him off her.

Somehow, the agile bastard landed on his feet, albeit a little wobbly. She swung, putting all her strength into her arm as it crashed against his temple, catching him off-guard. He toppled, and she leapt over him, raining blows down on his face relentlessly until it was one, big, swollen mess.

He spat blood at her. "He's dead!"

She froze, trying to search his eyes for the truth, but they were nearly puffed shut. "You lie!"

He managed an ugly smile before closing his eyes and passing out.

"No!" She shook him. Nothing. She pulled him up by his collar. "If he's dead, then you're next, you bastard." She picked his big body up and slammed him onto the ground. Once. Twice. She lost count. She screamed and yelled at the unconscious body she was most likely killing but didn't care. First her father is taken from her for no fucking reason. And now, Charlie? What the hell did the universe have against her? She snarled as she gazed down at Jaxon's unrecognizable face, roaring as she smashed her boot onto his face, hearing another satisfying crunch.

"Nessie?"

Her boot hung mid-air over Jaxon's face. Spinning, her eyes

darted over the landscape. Was her mind playing tricks on her already? Or had she just heard...

Her vision zoned in, landing on Charlie's sweet face and noticing the claw marks across his face and chest. Relief washed over her like a warm breeze in a blizzard, and she felt herself shrinking back to her normal form. In the distance, Charlie limped at Talon's side. She ran towards him. Reaching him a moment later, she cupped his face as she felt tears trickle down her cheeks. Jaxon lied. She sent up a silent apology to the universe. Maybe it wasn't all bad.

"He said you were dead," she croaked as she stroked his face. "I thought I'd never see you again."

He smiled at her. That stupid, aggravating, lopsided smile that annoyed her to no end was the most beautiful thing she'd ever seen. "And, obviously, that upset you?" He motioned towards Jaxon's unconscious body. "You aren't gonna get rid of me that easily."

She half-cried, half-laughed as she pulled him against her body. "Don't ever disappear on me like that again."

He wrapped his arms around her, holding her tight. She could smell the blood on his body, a mixture of his and several lycans. "I didn't disappear intentionally, I promise."

She pulled back to look at his face. "I know, I know. It's my fault. I shouldn't have bolted. I was so scared of everything. Acting like a pathetic fool."

He cupped her face in one palm, smiling down at her. "You just ran headfirst into a pack of angry lycans for me. I wouldn't call that scared or pathetic. Maybe a little foolish, though." He winked at her.

She slid her hand over his face. "I would've taken on ten packs for you."

His smile faded as his eyes widened. "Does this mean?"

Her eyes found the mark she had indeed left on his shoulder, running her fingers across the puckered skin. "It would seem I have officially claimed you."

His glanced down at his shoulder, his mouth falling open. "You...you...marked me." He snapped his gaze back to her.

"I didn't even know it, but I guess when a vampire falls in love with you, it's inevitable."

His lips crushed against hers in a kiss that shattered her thoughts, putting other kisses to shame. She wanted to fall into it and let it consume her...

Talon cleared his throat, pulling her back to reality where dozens of furry not-so-little monsters were waiting to rip them to pieces. "We should probably get back to Whitemoon now that Charlie's been recovered."

"Yeah," she and Charlie said in unison as they disentangled themselves.

"Absolutely," she said, her voice breathier than she intended.

"Let's go." Charlie's husky voice had her catching his gaze as they shared a sly smile, their gazes already darkening.

They made it to the basement in record time, not even bothering to wait until they were through the door. Nessie tugged at Charlie's shirt, contemplating ripping it off him. What the hell. It was stained with blood and dirt anyway.

Talon's chuckle mingled with the sound of what was left of Charlie's shirt being torn from his body. "I think we may have to remodel that basement soon," he murmured as he headed off toward a different part of the house.

Charlie kicked the door shut before Talon had finished speaking, pulling Nessie into a kiss to rock the gods right off their pedestals.

A chorus of rips and tears filled the room as clothes left bodies in a scramble of who could get the other naked first. Nessie won, having had a head start, but no victory dance ensued as Charlie pushed her onto the bed and tore her final piece of clothes (damn, and she liked those jeans) off her.

She plunged down on him as her fangs sank into his throat, groaning as he filled her up in so many ways. She released a muffled cry as he bit into her chest, marking her again, claiming her heart.

My heart was dead. Until I found you.

And my soul was caged. Until you set me free.

AUTHOR'S NOTE

Thank you so much for reading BITTEN BY DARKNESS. I hope you enjoyed the ride (I know I did writing it - most of the time). If you did, please consider leaving a review on Amazon or Goodreads.

These two were my first couple in this series, so they'll always have a special place in my heart. Turn the page to read an excerpt from Torin's book. His and Autumn's story tugged at a few heartstrings as I wrote it. Happy reading!

THE FORBIDDEN FATE SERIES

TEMPTED
BY
TWILIGHT

PROLOGUE

*S*OMETHING'S WRONG, SHE THOUGHT AS SHE STARED UP AT her mother's pale face. Her mother shivered in the damp, cold air of the cell they'd been thrown in several hours ago. She rubbed her hands over the bruises that blotched her mother's arms.

"Are you cold, mommy?" she asked, and her mother smiled down at her, running her fingers over her own cheek.

"No, baby, I'm fine," her mother whispered as her body shook again. She wanted to ask one of the guards for a blanket or coat to wrap around her mother, but, even in her short life, she knew better than to ask. It was a dangerous gamble. Some guards took pity on them, and some...didn't, to say the least. Her mother had been punished one too many times for her own mistakes, and, given her mother's fragile state, she didn't want to risk it again.

She continued to rub her mother's arms to stop the shaking.

Her mother forced her arms away as she went into a coughing fit again. It had been happening more and more often over the past few weeks, each time lasting longer and sounding worse. She wrapped her arms around herself as she watched her mother struggle to catch her breath. When her mother's hoarse gasps wrenched the air, she clapped her hands over her ears, blocking out the sound that made her feel helpless.

Closing her eyes, she plopped on the ground and rocked in place, humming loudly. Mommy's fine. Mommy said she's fine.

She didn't know her mother finally recovered until she knelt in front of her, pulling her arms from her ears. "I'm sorry, baby. I'm all better now," she murmured in her soft, lyrical tone.

Opening her eyes, she gazed up at her mother, finding her managing a weak smile. "You always say that," she said, frowning.

Guilt instantly clawed at her as her mother's small smile faltered for a moment. "I'm sorry, mommy," she muttered, watching as tiny wrinkles appeared on her mother's forehead before the woman grabbed hold of her and wrapped her up in her arms.

She sighed, snuggling closer into the cradle of her mother's body, wanting to share her warmth. Her mother rested her cheek on the top of her head. For long moments, they sat in silence, but then, her mother's voice broke the silence as she started to sing her favorite lullaby. She closed her eyes, letting her mother's beautiful voice wash over her, taking her away. There were tiny cracks in her mother's voice, though, reminding her of her mother's current condition.

Eventually, as her mother continued to rock and sing to her, exhaustion overtook her, and she fell asleep with her ear pressed against her mother's chest, listening to the irregular beats of her mother's heart.

"Get up, girls," one of the guards called from the other side of the cell, waking her sometime later. "It's time," he said, glancing at her mother with a face full of pity.

Nodding, her mother brushed her hair from her face. "Time to get up, baby." Groaning, she climbed from the warm bubble of her mother's embrace and stood up, offering a hand to her mother. Smiling, her mother took her hand and she helped pull her up. "My sweet girl," she said, kissing her cheek. "Thank you."

The guard led them out of the cell and out into the sunlight. Eyes widening at the scene before her, she clung a little tighter to her mother's side, who threw her arm around her shoulders and gave a squeeze. A crowd comprised of mostly men stood in front of a large wooden stage shouting at each other and the people on the stage, who happened to be mostly women and young girls. Of the few men on stage, there were two guards and a man shouting back at the crowd.

Still clinging to her mother's side, they followed the guard closer to the stage, her heart hammering harder and harder with each step. She felt her mother squeeze her a little tighter, hearing her sniffle. She didn't have to look up to know her mother was crying. She heard her cry before when she was supposed to be sleeping. But she didn't blame her. It was a sad life, raising a child alone and having men tell you what to do all day long. Life would be much better without those vile, smelly creatures.

As the guard led them up the steps of the stage, a knot formed in her stomach making her feet uncooperative. She stumbled several times, her mother catching her so she didn't fall on her face in front of the crowd. When the dozens of male faces turned in their direction, staring, snickering, and muttering amongst themselves, she completely froze. Her feet absolutely refused to take another step. She tried to step back, wanting to rush back down the steps and to the safety of the cell, but her mother held tight.

"No, baby. You have to stay here," she whispered as the man on stage began yelling. "Next up. Two females, a mother-daughter pair. Irish descent, so possibly some Celtic genes, rare, indeed."

Her mother continued to struggle to keep her on the stage when she wanted nothing to do with these people. Why couldn't they go back to the cell until this was over? The men in the crowd watched them closely, their eyes narrowing as her mother began coughing, begging her to stop. When her mother finally released her to fall to her knees in another coughing and gasping fit, she debated making a run for it. The men's voices grew louder as they talked amongst themselves. One of the men closest to the stage sneered in her mother's direction as she wheezed, and then snapped his gaze to her when she took several steps toward the stairs.

"Baby, no," her mother croaked through her coughs. Guilt racked her as she glanced back at her mother as she lay on the stage reaching for her. She couldn't do it. She couldn't just leave her mother lying there...all alone.

She rushed over, placing a gentle hand on her mother's back as it shook. "I'm sorry, mommy," she whispered. Her mother managed to glance at her before she began sobbing through her gasps, tears suddenly pouring from her beautiful eyes that matched the trees during her favorite time of year.

The men began yelling, and she moved her body in front of her mother, giving the nasty creatures in the crowd a look just as nasty. *What mean things they are*, she thought as she pet her mother's back.

"I'll take the girl," a low, booming voice suddenly came from the crowd. Her eyes searched the crowd, quickly finding the man (more like giant) parting the mass of men like the Red Sea. They bumped into each other to make room for him, the incessant muttering continuing. The hair on the back of her neck stood up as he approached the stage in long strides that ate the distance in a matter of seconds. Watching her with dark eyes, his lips curved into a smile. She found herself leaning back against her mother's body to move away from his approach.

"Sold!" the man on the stage shouted quickly.

The giant glanced away from her to look at the man on stage and her lungs began operating again. "I'll pay half the asking price for just the girl."

The man on stage frowned. "I'm sorry, but they are to be sold together."

Crossing his massive arms over his even more massive chest, the giant huffed. "I'm not paying for a woman who is obviously sick and possibly dying. And I doubt anyone else will either. It's the girl alone, or you can keep them." There were shouts of agreement from the crowd.

The man on stage spoke to Jevon, their current owner, in a hushed conversation for a moment before returning to the stage. "Very well," he said, nodding at the giant.

Those two words made her heart stop. Dead still. And when the man's eyes turned back to her, his smile widening, she wished she could stay and die with her mother.

"No!" her mother screamed, somehow finding the strength to stand despite gasping for air. Yanking her behind her, her mother stood glaring up...way up...at the giant who was quickly bearing down on her. "You...can't...have...her," she managed, narrowing her eyes on him. "I know...what you...are."

The smile on the giant's face never faltered as his eyebrow quirked in amusement. "Oh, I'd love to see your sweet, sickly ass try to stop me," he murmured and chuckled at her.

She remained there, staring at him, her eyebrows furrowed until finally she lowered her head, her shoulder slumping. Turning, her mother knelt clutching her shoulders. "I'm so sorry, baby. I should have let you run."

Her eyes widened as her gaze darted from her mother to the giant towering behind her. When her eyes landed on the giant's smirking face, she started shaking her head. "No, mommy," she pleaded, her head shaking faster. "No, please don't let them take me."

Tears streamed from both of them as her mother wrapped her up in her arms. "I love you, baby. I will always love you."

Huffing, the giant stepped forward, his boots pounding against the hollow, wooden floor of the stage. "Time to go, girl," he snapped, clutching her arm and yanking her from her mother's arms in one, quick jerk. She screamed, turning enough to pummel her free fist against the arm that clutched her own. Kicking her feet, she refused to walk away from her mother. When he picked her up, she swiped her hand over his face, scratching his cheek open. He chuckled, and threw her over his shoulder, where she continued kicking and pounding on his back with every ounce of strength her tiny body possessed.

"I like this one already," he said as she noticed a second pair of boots fall into step beside his enormous ones.

"Nadene will have that beaten out of her in a month," the second man said, making her pause for a moment before resuming her struggle tenfold. *Gods, who are these people?!*

CHAPTER ONE

Sixteen years later...

GAZING AROUND THE BARE TWELVE BY TWELVE ROOM, Autumn sighed heavily. Why was she here? Couldn't it just be over already? She'd suffered enough, hadn't she? She glanced down at the bowls of paint that littered the hardwood floor. Jaelyn, the only person in this god-forsaken world she didn't absolutely despise, snuck the bowls of paint in with her daily meal. Turning her head, a smile of minuscule proportions crossed her face as she admired her latest piece. It took up a solid three square feet of wall space that had once been pristine white. Once again, she had depicted the woman that haunted her dreams for as long as she could remember. Long, flowing locks of red, ivory skin, and piercing eyes of jade with ugly streaks of tears blotching her beautiful face.

Now, with her mind no longer engrossed in her painting, she noticed the slight shivering of her body and the goosebumps that covered her skin. Gathering the bear fur blanket around her, she curled into a ball on her side. When she heard the stampeding of feet and paws rush past outside, shouts and howls soon joining the chaos, she clamped her hands over her ears. Gods, it wasn't even the full moon yet. She waited for them to pass, as they always did, as the cluster of men raced into the forest to hunt. But they didn't. She clenched her teeth, her hands failing to block them out. Finally, after forever passed, she huffed and got to her feet, padding over to the tiny window draped in bear fur. And what she saw had her jaw dropping.

Dozens of men and wolves cluttered the spaces between the houses and buildings of Blackmoon, teeth bared and snapping, fists clenched and swinging. It was an all-out battle as she saw several men bleeding, and a few wolves trying to limp away. She watched entranced for long minutes, trying to puzzle out what had happened to cause such a fight to break out. Did it really matter? If anything, it may be just the distraction she needed.

Throwing the blanket off her, she leapt toward the door. This was it. Time to get out of this hellhole. She yanked on the doorknob, cursing when she found it locked. Nadene, her witch of a caretaker, had probably locked it after throwing her in at dusk. She added her other hand, pulling harder. Nothing. Slamming a fist, she let her head fall on the door...a little harder than she meant to. C'mon, door. Budge. She wouldn't get another chance like this. She had never witnessed a battle like this happen within the village. Even he (she shuddered even thinking his name) would be too preoccupied to notice her escape. She had to do it...NOW!!!! So, cooperate, you stupid thing!

She ran across the room, taking a deep breath before sprinting toward the door, her whole body slamming into it. A giant thud echoed through the room, but the door remained completely intact. Again. Harder this time. She could feel bruises forming on her right shoulder. But she wouldn't stop. This was her chance. And she'd beat her body bloody if it meant getting out of here.

Torin Delaney enjoyed a good sparring match as much as any other warrior, but these Blackmoon bastards fought dirty. Growling as yet another Blackmoon shifted, he gripped the hilt of his short sword. Typical Blackmoon, he thought. They always relied on their wolf forms it seemed. The first wolf barreled down on him, baring its ugly yellow teeth at him. He clipped it on the shoulder as he dodged out of the way. It yelped. It was a risky move bringing a silver sword into battle, given that he could quite literally be killed with his own sword. He allowed himself a grin of satisfaction as the wolf snarled at him for the injury. Shouldn't have shifted so quickly, dumbass.

He nipped the mutt a few more times as they played a little cat and mouse. Only this mouse had a sword, and some mad skills with it, if he did say so himself. When a familiar war cry rang through the air, he glanced to his left, shaking his head and smiling. *Alaric, you arrogant SOB.* His best friend carried a sword almost identical to his own, and Torin knew the man could use it. As evidenced by the several scars he had from when the prick nicked him with it during "training." Alaric slashed at one of the wolves in a smooth upward motion, grinning over at him.

"Couldn't keep away I see," he yelled to him. Despite Pop's warning, he thought. His father, the Alpha, didn't like Alaric joining battles for the simple fact that he was human, and believed that immediately gave Alaric a disadvantage. However, Torin had taught his best friend everything he knew. And what Pop didn't know wouldn't hurt him.

"Couldn't let you have all the fun," Alaric yelled back, winking as he took the wolf's legs out from under him.

Chuckling, Torin returned to the snarling dog in front of him. "If Pop sees you, the fun will be over...for both of us." The tip of his sword sank into the meat of the wolf's shoulder, drawing a high-pitched shriek from the animal as its leg gave out.

Bang. Torin paused as he was about to gut the wolf a second time. Bang. Looking through the small crowd of wolves and his Whitemoon brothers, he couldn't figure out who was causing the sound. Bang. He followed the sound to a small building near the edge of the village. Bang. What the? It sounded as if someone was being thrown against the door. Bang. Closing in on the building, he peered through the window, astonished at what he found.

The source of the loud banging was a small woman...throwing herself against the door. He watched in awe as she stumbled to the opposite side of the room and ran headlong into the door. There were already some nasty-looking bruises forming on the right side of her body. Her right cheek was scratched open, and she had blood trickling down her arm. She was going to beat herself to a bloody pulp soon. He pounded on the glass, catching her attention, her eyes widening as she froze. "Stay there," he said through the glass. She just stared at him, unmoving. Well, she'd stopped throwing herself at the door, at least. He stepped over to the door, and, not hearing any more banging, proceeded to slam his boot into it. Solid as it was, though, it took a few kicks to get it to come crashing down. He stepped over the scattered pieces of wood, finding her flattened against the opposite wall, inching her way toward the corner.

Her face was an orchestra of color. Bruises, blood, and... paint? An array of colors streaked across the smooth alabaster skin, every bit as beautiful as the painting on the wall behind her. Her wide-set eyes just as bright as the woman in the painting. A self-portrait perhaps? Wild tangles of red hair haloed her face with still more paint streaked through it. Huddled in the far corner of the room, she stared at him with eyes like glimmering emeralds, biting her bottom lip, which happened to be one of the few spots on her face that were not splotched with paint. No, instead, they were pale pink, plump, and ... perfect. With his eyes locked on her face, he noticed a light dusting of freckles across her nose.

He took a step toward her, and she shrank back against the wall as if trying to will herself to disappear within the wooden panels. He raised his hands in plain sight continuing toward her. She watched him, trembling like a cornered animal. Pity and fierce determination seized him. He had to save her. Pain, pure and palpable, peered from the depths of her unblinking gaze. Terror radiated from her trembling body. What had this girl gone through to warrant such a reaction to a complete stranger?

"It's okay. I'm not gonna hurt you." He spoke softly trying not to scare her even worse than he obviously already had. "What's your name?"

Her eyes widened further turning into giant saucers on her slender face. Tiny shakes of her head told him she wouldn't be answering the simple question. Her eyes darted to the door as the screams and shouts from the battle that still raged grew louder. He was running out of time, he realized as he glanced out the small window. He turned back to face her, taking a breath before holding his hand out. She plastered herself against the wall, still shaking her head. "I know you're scared, but if you want out of here, it's now or never." He drilled his gaze into her, needing her to comprehend the urgency of the situation. "I'll give you to the count of five. After that, I'm gone, and I'll assume you'd rather stay here."

He started counting.

Oh, Gods, he was going to leave. Her mind spun in turmoil. He was one of those vile creatures she had come to despise more and more over the years, but he was offering to take her away from here. Away from this sad, lonely existence where she sat in this small room and spoke to no one. Just her and her paint as she wondered when the monster of a man would visit her next. A never-ending sea of terror that she drowned in day after day. And he was offering her a lifesaver.

"Suit yourself. I'm outta here," he snapped, turning on his heel toward the door. Her body stood and rushed over to him, falling into step beside him. He glanced over at her, and she saw his mouth curve in a tiny smile as he nodded. She gulped. Men smiling were never a good thing in her world. It usually came before they did something unspeakable. She was about to run back to the corner when he headed for the doorway, cracking the door open. He turned back to her, whispering, "Stay close to me, gorgeous."

Gorgeous? What did that mean? He held his hand out again, as if he meant for her to take it. She inched her way over to him, stepping around his arm. He quirked his brow at her before shrugging. "Suit yourself." Out the door he went, and she hurried after him.

She gasped as the sharp cold air hit her. She'd left the blanket inside, and she didn't own a pair of shoes. The ground stung her feet as she stepped through the snow the blizzard had left a few days ago. She followed him as best she could as he weaved around buildings, trying to avoid the crowd of men engaged in battle. And then, she saw him. The monster trudged easily through the snow, and she gasped, throwing her hands over her mouth to muffle the sound. *Please, don't see me. Please, don't see me.* To be mauled by that monster again after being so close to escape...

Her rescuer halted a few feet in front of her as she gasped, turning back to look at her. She hadn't realized she had frozen in place, her eyes following the monster as he made a beeline around some smaller buildings in the distance. He was on the hunt for his next victim, she saw it in the hard stare of his soulless eyes. As he rounded a corner and disappeared, she let out a huge sigh of relief.

"Shit, I should have noticed how poorly you were dressed for this weather." Returning her attention to the man taking her away from the monster, she tilted her head as he stripped off his heavy coat and moved towards her. She cringed as his fingers brushed her shoulder, placing the warm garment across her shoulders. He smiled at her again, this time more fully, and even though her heart raced at the sight, at least his smile didn't look completely maniacal. "Is that better?" he asked her. As if he cared about her comfort or something. She gave him a hesitant nod. Why in the world would he sacrifice his own warmth for her comfort? That didn't make any sense at all.

For some reason, his eyes fell along with his smile. Hmmmm... he looked much nicer with a smile on his face. She never thought she'd ever say that about a man. Most of the men that had ever smiled at her had been downright creepy...or straight-up evil. "Gods, they didn't give you a pair of shoes? I always knew Blackmoon could be real dicks, but this is ridiculous." Then, without warning, he just scooped her up.

She thrashed instantly, her body trembling at the thought of being touched. "Whoa, babe. Calm down." Yeah, fat chance. She pummeled him, hammering her fists against his chest. *Put me down, you caveman!* After several unsteady steps, he finally set her on her feet, and she bolted. *Can't let him touch me.*

When he fell into step beside her, easily keeping pace with

her, she tried to run in a different direction, but everything looked the same. All tall trees, bushes, and snow. Not that she would have had a clue where she was going otherwise.

"You know, I could do this all day. But, for the sake of time...and your feet, it would be a lot easier if you let me lead. You don't have shoes, so I'm guessing you don't really have anywhere to go either."

Slowing, she glanced over at him, finding him watching her while somehow not running into anything. Finally, she stopped, hunching over clasping her thighs as she tried to catch her breath. Being locked in that building when she wasn't cleaning clothes or weaving baskets, meant she was not a runner by any means. He crouched down, gazing up at her and smirking. "Ready to let me carry you yet?" he asked, wiggling his eyebrows.

Her jaw dropped. Was he crazy? He certainly didn't look crazy...and she'd seen crazy. His eyes were soft and warm, like a crackling fire with shades of copper, green, and honey tones. The longer she stared, the more colors seemed to pop out at her from the depth of his eyes. She shook her head between gasping for air. Tiny lines appeared at the corners of those multi-colored eyes as he smiled again, chuckling. He drove a hand through his short, blonde hair, lifting a shoulder. "Ah, well. I tried."

Her neck cracked as she tilted her head to the side again. This guy confused the hell out of her. What was his angle? He helps her escape. He gives her his big, warm coat. He offers to carry her. Why? What did he get out of this?

"I'd hate to see you lose a toe," he said, now removing his shoes. Seriously? What was wrong with him? She shook her head furiously at him. *Stop giving me your stuff, you weirdo!* "No, really. Here. I'll at least have socks." She shook her head again. He rolled his eyes, huffing and thrusting the pair of boots into her arms. She stumbled back, staring up at him. "Just put them on," he snapped, crossing his arms over his chest as he waited.

Another few moments of her frozen body staring at him. He jutted a finger at the boots. "Before your toes fall off, babe."

She furrowed her brows at his stupid nickname. He gave her a droll look. "Either put those damn boots on, or I'm carrying you whether you like it or not."

She sucked in a breath before narrowing her gaze on him as she pulled her snow-covered foot up to slip the boot on. Her tiny feet swam in them, but her frozen toes thanked him even if she didn't.

He nodded. "That's what I thought." He turned and began trekking through the snow. She stuck her tongue out at his back and trudged along after him.

Something was wrong with this woman. He didn't know what, but there had to be a reason for her touchiness. He found himself stealing glances at her as she walked beside him. His coat engulfed her lithe body, the scrap of a dress she wore hidden beneath it, and his boots flopped every time she took a step. Some very male part of him got an immense sense of satisfaction seeing his clothes consuming her tiny body. His eyes finally crept upwards...oh, shit. Busted.

Her eyes drilled into him, eyebrow quirked, lips pursed. Not uttering a word, but her face screamed, *Okay, creeper, knock it off...like now!*

He averted his gaze, looking at anything but her. The silence stretched, feeling awkward. "So," he started. "You never did tell me your name?" He risked a glance her way. She bit her bottom lip, drawing his gaze to them. She looked away, and he snatched the opportunity to study her face. Despite the marks that covered her skin, there was no denying she was attractive. Copper, mahogany, and bright auburn hair shimmered in the moonlight, reaching past her hips. Ivory skin, high cheekbones that were flushed pink from the cold. Small, perky nose with tiny freckles dotting across it. Bright, round eyes framed by a mass of dusky lashes. And those lips...those were what dreams were made of.

She glanced over at him, and he snapped his head away, whistling softly. He caught her rolling her eyes. "You do have a name, don't you?" he asked.

Giving him a haughty look, she nodded. As if it was unthinkable that she wouldn't have a name. He shrugged at her. "Well, you didn't answer, so how was I supposed to know?"

She contemplated that for a moment, and then simply shrugged back. He shook his head and returned his eyes to the path in front of him. "Big talker aren't ya," he mumbled, eliciting another roll of her eyes.

They walked for a while in silence. She seemed to be fascinated by the simplest things. She watched squirrels scurrying up trees with wide-eyed wonder. "By the way, that painting didn't do you justice." She snapped her head up to him, head tilted, eyebrows quirked. He chuckled. "I mean, you're much prettier in person than in that painting." Her cheeks reddened even more at the compliment. Pressing a hand against her chest, she shook her head.

"What? You didn't paint it?" She nodded. "You did paint it?" She nodded again. "Well, don't get me wrong. The painting is beautiful." He leaned a little towards her and she immediately leaned away. "But you're more beautiful in person."

Her cheeks flushed again as she shook her head. Apparently, she didn't like compliments. He raised his hands. "Okay, fine. I won't compliment you anymore." She let out a sigh and turned away, her hands flying. She stumbled, and he shot out an arm to catch her. She fell into him, her face pushing against his chest. She gazed up at him for a moment, and he smiled. "A little clumsy I see," he murmured.

Eyes wide, she flew out of his arms, pushing against his chest and swiftly landing on her backside in the snow. He chuckled and went to offer her a hand up. She scurried back, snow flying as she shook her head violently. He pulled his hand back. "Whoa, whoa, babe. Okay, okay. You can get yourself up. I get it. Calm down."

But she didn't seem to hear him, as she clamped her eyes shut and kept moving away from him, her head continually shaking. He followed her at a safe distance, not wanting to make her freak out again. Then, her eyes popped open, and she stopped. Her eyes fluttered as her head lolled. Oh, shit.

He crouched next to her, catching her head as her eyes fluttered closed. Something warm and wet coated his hand. He pulled his hand away from the back of her head enough to see it smeared in blood. Oh, double shit!

He scooped her up and started running.

THE FORBIDDEN FATE SERIES
TEMPTED
BY
TWILIGHT

released (or will release) on November 12, 2021

Please visit <u>www.nicholewolfe.com</u> for information on how to order your copy for only $1.99 during pre-release.

NEWSLETTER SIGNUP

Don't forget to sign up for my newsletter at www.nicholewolfe.com to get a free e-book copy of BITTEN BY DARKNESS to keep on your favorite e-reader device.

If you're already signed up for my newsletter, thank you! I hope you enjoy your free e-book and stay tuned for more updates, discounts, and exclusive giveaways.

ABOUT THE
AUTHOR

NICHOLE WOLFE lives in a small village in Pennsylvania with her high school sweetheart, their two children, and several furbabies. When not working on her endless author to-do list, she can be found cooking for her family, gardening, eating at her favorite Italian restaurant, and haunting her local Dunkin Donuts. Find out more about her at her website, www.nicholewolfe.com.